TORRIE

By the same authors:

THE BLACK SYMBOL

TORRIE

by ANNABEL and EDGAR JOHNSON

HARPER & BROTHERS
Publishers NEW YORK

TORRIE

To

EVELYN AND BUNNY JONES

*Who looked for—and discovered—
a golden shore*

JANUARY

IT WAS a dark day with a swift sky—weather moving in. Time moving in. A new year coming on fast, two days old now, and already full of forebodings.

In the warm shadowy depths of the old barn behind the farmhouse, a girl stood at one of the small single-paned windows and stared out at the bleak sky and empty snow-drifted fields. She was slender, almost delicately thin, with such clear transparent skin that her wide-set eyes seemed shockingly dark. Her hair was sable brown too, plaited in two neat braids that fell down her back to her waist—fine-grained soft hair, unswervingly straight. The way she wore it, brushed evenly away from the center part, gave her a prim neatness that was oddly at variance with the fierce perplexity of her expression. The face itself . . .

Plain-faced. That was what some of the other girls called her. Torrie drew back a little from the window so that she could catch a dim glimpse of her reflection in the glass. She saw the same high-boned, strongly defined features that looked back at her every day from the mirror, although now, etched faintly against the clear glass and the roiling sky beyond, the image did take on a faint air of borrowed mystery.

Some inner crystal gave back a secret picture—of a mysterious beautiful woman waiting in a hidden garden for a handsome dark-visaged stranger who would drop to his knees at her feet and humbly kiss the hem of her velvet robes. . . .

Torrie gripped the frame of the window with both hands as if she'd like to shake it loose and smash it! And, as if it weren't bad enough to be homely and skinny, to be burdened with peculiar parents was just the last straw. Why couldn't they be like everybody else's parents? Fathers were supposed to be big and hearty and full of jokes, extra fond of their only daughters. And mothers— every mother she knew—they were all sweet and pleasant and soft-looking. They smelled faintly of perfume and spoke in gentle voices. This wasn't asking much—not much at all!

Furthermore, other people's parents at least made an effort to behave in such a way that their children would be proud of them. They didn't come up with wild—absolutely crazy—ideas, such as this California notion.

She looked across at the old man who sat on a barrel, mending harness, beside the only other window in the barn. If she hadn't had Grandpa this last year, Torrie thought, she'd have just died. Even if he was seventy-seven and far too old to understand most things, he listened to her. He really listened—she could talk and he'd talk back plainly, just one person to another. None of Mother's scolding or Father's lecturing. It seemed that always at home she was either being put off or told "no" to whatever she wanted. Always such arguments! But here at the farm it was peaceful. When a person wanted to be quiet, Grandpa could be still for hours. He was the only grown person Torrie knew who could do this. Oh, not like Father's kind of quiet—he just went blank to the world when he got engrossed in a book or something. But Grandpa was companionable about it, as if he were thinking the same sort of things she was.

Right now, he looked up at her as if they'd just been having a conversation. "You frettin' about this plan of your pap's?" he asked.

Torrie surged over to stand near him, her narrow back braced against the wall of the barn. "Don't you think it's utterly ridiculous?" she demanded. "Wanting to go off into a foreign country like California, with Indians and rattlesnakes and things? And after you get there, the people don't even speak English!"

"I dunno." The old man squinted up at her, his sunburned eyes bright as two pinpoints of blue flame under the shaggy white brows. "When I come out here to St. Louis forty years ago, you wouldn't believe it, baby, but they didn't speak nothin' except French and Spanish. You can git along."

"But this was American soil!" Torrie tossed her hands impatiently. "Besides that was *then*. This is 1846, Grandpa. It's time everybody acted civilized!"

"You implyin' your grandma and me wasn't?" He grinned.

Torrie felt herself color up. "No, of course not, but in those days even civilized people had to lead a—an unusual life sometimes. I mean, like living in a covered wagon and all that—it was even kind of romantic in those days. But

3

now, can you imagine us living like that? Mother? And *Father?*"

"Your ma lived in that wagon once when she was five years old." The old man glanced with a sort of affection toward the huge ancient vehicle that stood in the far corner of the barn. "That's still a good old cart, baby. She's a con-sarned fine sight too, with new canvas blazin' white in the sun and some strong oxen leanin' into the pull. She'll get you to—wherever you're goin'." He broke off. "Last I heard, your pa was thinkin' about Oregon."

"Oh, he doesn't know where he wants to go." Torrie twitched with exasperation. "He's found out that Oregon is rainy, so now he has another book, all about how wonderful California is. It's by some man named 'Hasty' or—"

"Hastings." Her grandfather nodded. "I read some of it myself, feller at the store had a copy the other day. It makes all that warm weather out there sound pretty good, don't it?"

"No!" she denied vehemently. "I like St. Louis. I like our house. I don't see why Father's suddenly got seized with this foolish—" Torrie checked, because even Grandpa had the old-fashioned idea that young girls shouldn't criticize their elders.

He took it tolerantly this time though. All he said was, "Easy does it, baby."

Baby! The word gritted Torrie's soul. "Grandpa," she said with strained dignity, "I am not a child any more. I am fourteen-and-a-half years old and that's nearly a woman grown."

He glanced up at her, quick and sober-faced. "Yes, ma'am, I reckon. I'll call you 'Miss Victoria' after this." Then gravely he added, "Is that what's makin' you so

4

prickly these days, bein' fourteen?"

She knew he was teasing and she ought not to answer him at all, but Grandpa teased people because he loved them—not to make fun, like that wretched little Caleb.

"I've got problems," she said earnestly. "A lot of very hard problems."

He studied the splice he'd made in the leather. "I been eatin' hard problems fer breakfast all my life," he said. "You get used to 'em, in the long run—if that's any comfort."

Torrie sighed and paced across the barn, her skirts switching around her ankles in angry little swirls. Coming up to the wagon, she clenched her hands and beat softly on its thick tailboard with her fists. It was an ugly old thing. Why Grandpa should ever have thought it fine-looking, she couldn't imagine. Big clumsy wooden wheels capped with heavy strips of iron. What an elegant way to travel!

Mournfully she thought of the ladies who drove their pretty little sulkies through the Park; she pictured an exquisitely dressed young woman holding the light reins in her gloved hands while two beautiful bay horses drew the carriage with its sparkling little wire-spoke wheels that rolled silently, smooth as butter. . . .

"Yes sir," Grandpa remarked behind her, "that schooner's made out of good Pennsylvania oak."

"But it's so old!"

"It's been took good care of all these years. Some things git better with age," he told her, with his warm old humor. "Hardwood's one of 'em. Applejack's another. Folks sometimes too. Few years can improve 'em. You take me"—he chuckled—"I git better all the time. That's because I keep my mouth shut and my eyes open."

5

"What do you think of my father?" Torrie asked boldly, eying him over her shoulder, daring him to reprove her for the question. "Is he getting better with age?"

"I dunno." The old man frowned at his leather. "It ain't easy to tell about somebody else. Your pa had the sense to buy that wagon from me and asked me to pick out his team for him, come auction day. I'd call that some bright. It ain't every man'll admit how much he *don't* know."

"But Father doesn't know practically everything," Torrie told him, honestly. "I mean except what's in his books, and what good is that when he's so—so—unaware of people and their feelings and all?"

"Book learnin' is one of the other things I ain't sure about." Grandpa shook his head. "Never had enough to tell. But your pa ain't held the fact against me, I'll say that. And so long as your ma ain't complainin' . . ."

"Oh, Mother!" Torrie kicked at the wheel of the wagon, blunting her toe on it smartly. But she couldn't say to *him* all that was in her mind about Mother.

The fact was—and they needn't think it was such a secret—Mother was lucky to have got married at all. She was plain-faced and big, and she hadn't even had any offers until she was over twenty-four years old, which meant she was practically a spinster. Only an absent-minded little man like Father would have considered her even of use as a housekeeper—which was all he'd evidently wanted. Torrie had known for years how little her parents really cared for each other; they never acted close or even friendly, although Father was completely polite, of course, and called her "my dear" in a perfunctory way. And if Mother didn't complain to Grandpa, it certainly wasn't because she was happy. Torrie could hardly remember the time there hadn't

6

been a little frown on her mother's face and a sharp tone of scolding in her voice. Not that she ever was outright cross with Father, but it was just impossible to imagine them ever being in love.

Of course Torrie really felt very sorry for them, but she was not going to let them ruin her life. If they had this notion to go to California, then let them, but they weren't going to drag her along, especially just now when she was getting old enough to start going out socially. Practically ever since she could remember, Torrie had been thinking of her first dance.

She hoped there would be a young man in uniform, even a cadet from the new Naval Academy in the East. He'd come up and bow before her. . . . Will you do me the honor to be my partner in the cotillion, oh, beautiful one . . . ?

She turned desperately to confront Grandpa again. "Don't you think it's downright cruel of parents not to let their grown daughter go to the Twelfth Night Ball?"

"Depends. Was their daughter asked?"

"That's not the point. Mother said I couldn't go even if I *were* invited."

He didn't say anything for a minute.

Encouraged, Torrie rushed on with some of the injustices that had been bottled up for so long. "She's so unreasonable! She won't let me put my hair up—can you imagine? All the others girls I know wear their hair up, but Mother doesn't like the girls I go with. She's always finding fault—she made me stay in all last week when everybody was out sleigh-riding!"

"I thought that was because you had a chill," he remarked.

"Oh, who cares about a chill! It wasn't a very bad one. I missed half of the Christmas fun. I think she enjoys making me miserable." Torrie came back to his side and sank down unhappily onto a pile of clean straw nearby. "And Father never takes my part, not even once. I don't think he even knows I'm alive. I know he always wanted all his children to be boys—he's so kind to Cal, you'd think Cal was a little angel. But me—" she crumpled up a handful of straw and flung it from her bitterly—"he doesn't give *that* for me."

"Sounds like you got problems all right," Grandpa said sympathetically. "Didn't know things was so bad."

"They've been getting worse. And now this wild-goose chase off into the wilderness, all of us cooped up in a wagon for months and months—I think my father's lost his mind!"

"Oh, not permanent," the old man assured her mildly. "It's a kind of passin' fever that takes hold of a man. I heard a dozen others say the same thing. Old Dan'l Boone, before he died, I remember it well, he was sittin' right over there on a keg of nails. He allowed as how it was a itch brought on by bein' crowded, all organized up with a mess of other folk into doin' the same thing, day in, day out. You get to need to bust a-loose and be alone, just wander off where you feel like and stop when you get good and ready. Maybe it ain't sensible but it's a strong feelin'. You get the wish to use yourself, try yourself out on new chores— somethin' to put your heart into. You get a hunch to go to new land, search it out, and grow somethin' on it—"

"But Father's a schoolteacher!"

Grandpa fell quiet and thoughtful. He couldn't answer that one. Of course maybe there was something to what he

8

said—Mother was certainly always looking for work to do, even making jobs for herself, sewing quilts they didn't need and putting up more jam than they could ever eat. She even seemed to like to worry, so maybe she'd enjoy this miserable trip, but Father just wasn't the type. He was content to read, or even just think. As recently as this past Christmas he had gone calmly about grading papers and preparing assignments for next term. And then practically the following day he had come up with the news that they were going to emigrate, as he called it. The only explanation he had given was that he'd been considering the move for some time. But it didn't make sense. All within a week he had found a teaching replacement and started studying all the books he could find on the western territories. There was something secret about it all, Torrie knew that much—something even sinister.

"Young people have hunches too," she told her grandfather distantly. "Some people mature much earlier than others—some people age fast when they've lived all their life with hardships. Some young people have more common sense than older ones."

"I wouldn't know, myself." Grandpa rubbed oil into the leather with his hard seamed old fingers. "When I was young, I was a plumb fool."

But Torrie hardly heard him as she leaned back into the straw. Some of the twisted-up-tight feeling inside her was miraculously easing, now that she'd made up her mind. Definitely. She wasn't going to California. She was going to run away.

FEBRUARY

ONCE THE decision was taken, Torrie's plans came to her as easily as daydreams. In fact, those first weeks it all seemed like an illusion, and Torrie had to remind herself from time to time what was going to happen. In two months or even less, she'd be free of the rules, the miserable restrictions—rid of being a child forever.

Almost at once it brought about a new self-possession. She was able to go ahead with good grace, pretending to get ready, working in the kitchen after lessons were done, helping put up corned beef and salt pork—she was a little amazed that her mother knew how to do such things. There'd never been any need to, here in the city. Now, though, the crocks of food began to pile up in the pantry— but even that didn't make the whole thing seem believable.

There was a tedious lot of sewing to be done, big dust covers to protect the few pieces of furniture that were to be taken, stitching endless flannel sacks for the silver— family silver that some day should have been Torrie's but which she wasn't ever going to see again. All the old familiar things, going—forever.

10

But whenever she got to feeling even the least regretful, she had only to go over in her mind all the benefits she would be gaining—the wonderful dignity of new-found freedom would come over her, and she felt strong enough for anything. There would be new people who would treat her as an adult, there'd be men and pretty clothes and garden parties next summer which she could attend whenever she chose to, without asking anyone's permission.

Her first new dress would be rustling sapphire taffeta—and of course she'd never wear braids again. Just wait —just wait until Grandpa saw her in curls piled up on top of her head!

For that was her plan; to go to live with Grandpa. Just as the others were leaving, she'd slip off and hide somewhere—she had enough allowance money saved to pay for a room at the hotel. Then as soon as they got tired of looking for her and went on, she'd simply go out to the farm. Grandpa must be lonesome there all by himself— she knew he'd be pleased to have her to cook for him. And he certainly would never forbid her to wear curls. So it was all working out quite easily. She had even chosen a fictitious name to give when she registered at the hotel. Delice Marlowe. It was about as different as possible from Victoria Anders. She thought she might even keep it permanently—she'd never thought much of Victoria, even if it was the name of the Queen of England.

And so her speculation rambled dreamily until, one evening in February, the whole thing abruptly became real.

They were all gathered around the fireplace after supper, Mother sewing, Caleb sitting cross-legged at her feet, scowling over the silver platter he was polishing—ten years old and disgusted to have to do "woman's work." And, by the bookcase, Father stood sorting through his library. With a twinge of nostalgia, Torrie thought this was the way she would remember them, always. . . .

Liza Anders was square-built and sturdy, her broad face just faintly sprinkled with fading freckles, the light sand-colored hair getting gray. The little frown was there as she bent over her work sewing the backing on a quilt, carefully stitching banknotes in between the two layers. It was so like Mother, Torrie thought, to go to such pains to hide their savings. One of her favorite remarks was, "Prudence saves pennies and pennies make pounds." She even looked prudent—it was in the set of her jaw.

She was irked right now at Cal. He'd been deviling them all evening about getting another horse, even though it had been made completely definite that they were fortunate to have one horse, which Grandpa had given them for Father to ride, and there was no extra money to buy another. As usual, it put the boy into a horrid mood. When he frowned he looked very much like his mother although his hair was a shade lighter, the freckles a good deal darker. But whereas Liza's look was set, Cal's face was restless and full of expressions that came and went at a stroke, transforming his features violently. Torrie detested him.

These last few weeks he'd been positively fiendish. The prospect of California had added fuel to his already raging fires—the energy the boy could put out left Torrie feeling exhausted. He never walked upstairs, he ran. He flung himself through the house clumsily, with a great racket, bumping into things, gulping his food, flying into rages and wild enthusiasms. And when he finally did get ordered to bed still seething with vitality, he'd fall asleep into such furious dreams that his thrashing around and groaning kept them all awake. She could just imagine what it would be like, trying to sleep in the same wagon with him and with Father, who snored.

She looked over at the man standing before the bookcase, just as he so often did, a volume open in his hand and all else forgotten as he scanned its pages through little gold-rimmed glasses. Thomas Anders was a slender man, almost brittle-looking. It was easy to see where Torrie had inherited her delicate build. Like her, he was dark too, although his hair was so thin it hardly disguised his bald spot anymore. And his eyes were the same dark brown as hers, but there the similarity ended. They were thoughtful eyes, judicial, remote, almost always impersonal. Even his emotions were the slow-burning kind that never quite reached the point of active excitement. And once his five senses turned inward in some contemplation, he was impervious to noise, color, or warmth—everything.

Right now, the pipe that he was fingering vacantly had gone out. Torrie supposed it was some poem that was engrossing him. He used to try to read them aloud to the whole family, but nobody listened. Poetry seemed so stupid. One of his favorites was something about a cow: "Forth, beast, out of thy stall!" What on earth—?

He glanced up now with a distant smile. "It's curiously comforting," he remarked, "to realize that other men hundreds of years ago felt the same impulses that motivate us today and set down their feelings to reach out across the centuries. Listen to this:

"Whenever April with her showers sweet
The drouth of March has pierced unto the deep. . . .
When small birds make their wild song as they fly,

(Though they must sleep all night with open eye,
So nature pricketh in each one a courage)
Then do men long to go on pilgrimage. . . ."

He looked around at them as if searching for the kindled spirit that he himself apparently felt. But Liza had gone on with her sewing, and Cal was scrubbing at the silver, ferociously plunged in his own private thoughts. Father looked at Torrie, but she couldn't understand what he might be thinking—it was as if she were staring at someone she hardly knew.

He closed the book and put it into the packing box. "I believe," he said, "that you all should know that the papers were signed on the sale of the house today. The new owner wishes to take possession before the end of March."

The calm statement brought them all to attention where the poetry had not. Torrie could see it taking effect on Cal and Mother, too—the realization that this house was not theirs any longer. A sudden choking emotion came over her. Not that the house was so handsome—a teacher's pay doesn't call for a big beautiful house—but it had been their home ever since she could remember. Besides, Torrie thought grimly, they'd be lucky if they got some ugly little log hut in California. Certainly nobody was going to hire Father to teach the Mexicans all about English literature. She wondered just what he thought he was going to do when he got out there. All at once, she hated him angrily.

Cal had rallied now. Bluffly he said, "The next house we get, I hope it's going to have a stable for my horse."

Nobody bothered to take issue with this—it would only have meant more argument. Mother had digested the news of the sale by now—it always took her longer.

14

"March'll be cold, no grazing for the stock, and the streams will be high from runoff, maybe get a blizzard, I'd say we should wait 'til mid-April." She always spoke that way, in a steady stream, as if to get the words out before she should get cut off, though no one ever cut her off.

Father nodded soberly. "You're correct in every instance, my dear, but there's better than two thousand miles to be traversed before next fall. I believe we'll be well advised to take our snows at this end rather than the other."

That settled it. Mother never argued with him.

But it meant there were only about three weeks to go! And it all finally got home to Torrie—painfully brilliantly real, the way a near stroke of lightning puts vivid edges on everything. It was true. They were going. And she was about to venture out into the world alone.

"Take care, there, Miss, you're sewing that seam almighty crooked and we don't have flannel to spare." Her mother's warning prodded Torrie out of her daze, and she tried to concentrate on what she was doing. Three weeks, though. Only three weeks. . . .

"Well, if I don't have a horse," hollered Caleb desperately, "at least I ought to have a gun! I'm going to *need* a gun!"

Father glanced up mildly. "By George, I almost forgot." He went across to his desk and searched in the drawer— Torrie could hardly believe her eyes when he straightened up, a pistol in his hand.

Caleb yipped with shrill ecstasy. Mother sat stock-still eying the weapon with its long wicked steel barrel glinting in the lamplight. It looked strange in Thomas Anders' hand—he held it rather gingerly as if it were some scientific specimen.

Cal had scrambled to his knees at his father's feet, visibly thirsting to touch the thing.

"No, Caleb, it's loaded," Thomas said gravely. "I don't want you to handle it until we're out in the open countryside. Then perhaps we'll all learn to use it."

Torrie swallowed down an impulse toward hysterical laughter. Liza set her lips and went back to her sewing.

"Grandpa's rifle always was plenty to bring home food," she commented flatly. "Caleb, are you going to get that platter rubbed up?"

"The rifle will still be the best gun for hunting game, my dear," Father told her politely. "But this weapon has a most ingenious feature—a mechanism which rotates this cylinder with every pull of the trigger so that, after each shot, a new cartridge revolves into place ready for the next firing. It's an innovation by a Mr. Samuel Colt—really an excellent invention if one is faced with the necessity for rapid fire."

"Like if Indians are coming over the top of the hill—" Cal screeched in mock alarm. "There's an Indian chief! Bam! Bam! I got 'im!" He went through a spasm of make-believe combat, but Thomas didn't even seem to notice the antics.

"For a small firearm," he was going on, as calmly as if he were lecturing his classes, "this shoots quite an impressive load." Laying the gun aside, he took from his pocket a handful of cartridges, each tipped with a blunt brutal leaden nose. Torrie felt sickly uneasy as she stared at them, gleaming dully in her father's palm. He must actually be expecting trouble, then. And this talk of Indians and panthers and buffalo—it wasn't all just the product of Cal's overheated imagination. She hadn't pictured her parents heading into actual danger. Everybody had heard about Comanches and Apaches, but it seemed so unlikely that you'd ever meet one in person. . . .

The room was rocked by a shattering blast! Half-deafened, stunned, Torrie leaped to her feet, scattering the sewing materials all over the floor. Mother was standing too, the quilt clutched in her hands. Father hadn't moved, but he had gone suddenly quite pale. All three of them stared at Caleb, who still held the gun stiffly in both hands as the pungent smell of burned powder drifted out across the room. He was staring down stupidly at the neat black hole where his accidental shot had torn through the floor.

Grinning uncertainly, he said, "The trigger pulls easy."

"Thomas—!" Mother's voice sounded slightly strangled. "If you don't punish that boy—!"

Father looked at her, troubled. To Cal he said in a quiet voice, "Put the gun down."

Sheepishly, Cal did as he was told and stood waiting for whatever blow might fall.

Torrie waited too—for some reason she was almost on the verge of nervous tears. The room still echoed with the terrible reverberations of that shot. The idiot child could have killed somebody. If Father didn't whip him this time—!

Thomas Anders looked around at them calmly. "I trust this experience has impressed upon all of you that it is not wise to handle an unfamiliar weapon." Then, seriously, he added, "However, it does provide us with an opportunity to assess the energy of the charge. I believe I'll just go down to the cellar and see if I can measure the degree of penetration—"

Torrie sank weakly into her chair. Oh, this was going to be a fine trip of theirs! She offered up a tremulous prayer of thanks that she wasn't going to be along to see what developed. Matters *couldn't* grow anything but worse.

MARCH

THERE WASN'T time for curls—and Torrie wasn't completely sure how to make them anyway. But it helped to coil the braids up on the nape of her neck in two thick rolls. Carefully, she settled the hat—Mother's wedding hat that had been in the attic all these years. When they'd been sorting out what was to go and what to be thrown away, Mother had looked high and low for that hat. Torrie had held her breath for fear someone would find it where she had hidden it. The dress was also one of Mother's—a Sunday dress with a lace panel in front and a high lace collar; it hadn't even been missed.

But of course the hat was the important thing. Not that white satin was exactly proper for March, but the full brim did wonders for her face, and the long feather was very impressive. Hesitating for one last look in the mirror, Torrie tried to imagine what impression she would make on the hotel clerk, especially so late at night.

Just maddening . . . my carriage has broken down and I can't go on to St. Genevieve where my poor aunt is ill

... must stay here in St. Louis a while ... do you have an inexpensive room?

She rehearsed it silently to the mirror. No use fooling herself, she didn't look very old. If only she could have got hold of some of the rouge that several of the girls used secretly when their mothers weren't around. It did make a person appear older even if it was a little cheap-looking.

Intently, Torrie chewed at her lips to see if she could bring color into them. Well, she thought, she had a perfectly genuine cough, so maybe they'd think she was slightly ill and let it go at that. She held the handkerchief to her face and coughed into it delicately. That was wonderful! It covered almost all the lower part of her face and made her eyes seem older. She thought: I must remember to feel old.

And then, as she turned for one last look at her room, she didn't have to manufacture the wistful expression—it came naturally. The place looked so empty. Some of the furniture had been packed into the wagon that stood below in the yard, the rest was sold. Only the bed was left, and a few last-minute things such as the mirror and lamp, the pitcher and basin. But the essence of it was gone, all the things she'd lived with ever since she was a baby.

Firmly she made herself stop thinking about that. Giving her hair one more pat, she put the comb and brush away in the little satchel of personals that was all she was going to take with her. Her dresses were all packed in the wagon, but it was just as well. She didn't intend ever to wear that type of thing again. Prudish calico dresses with high-buttoned collars and long sleeves, loose-fitting gingham pinafores—awful, unstylish clothes. Now this gown was better, especially since she'd pinned it up tight at the waist.

Even though she couldn't fill it out properly in front, at least it had a nice flare to the skirt—it must have been something Mother wore a long time ago when she was a girl. Torrie hadn't ever seen her dress prettily, so it must date back years.

As she put on the black wool cape, it looked quite proper with the dress, though it did make the hat seem terribly white by contrast. However, there wasn't anything she could do about that.

Tiptoeing to the door, she listened, but the house had been quiet for an hour. They'd all gone to bed early so as to be up at daybreak and get a good start—Father's idea. Turning down the lamp, Torrie took up her satchel and let herself out into the hall. Groping her way downstairs carefully, she managed to avoid the several treads that creaked—she had memorized them by heart—and reached the bottom without having made enough noise to be heard a foot away. There was a faint glow in the lower hallway where a lamp was always left burning low. It gave enough light for her to cross quickly to the door. Beginning to be a little frightened, heart pumping fast inside her, Torrie had a hand on the knob when a small—a very small—sound froze her in her tracks.

Someone was standing in the doorway of the study.

For a terrifying instant, Torrie stood transfixed, and then Father said quietly, "Don't be afraid, Victoria, it's only myself."

He went over to the small table where the lamp stood and busied himself for a minute, turning up the wick. It gave her a chance to try to collect herself . . . everything sinking inside her in wild hopeless defeat. . . .

"Let us go into the study." Thomas didn't seem par-

21

ticularly angry, but then he never lost his temper. It was one of the infuriating things about him—the way he could always preserve that inhuman coolness. Torrie walked ahead of him into the barren little room, its bookshelves empty, the furniture gone except for an old divan that they hadn't been able to sell to anyone. At her father's silent gesture, she sat down on it, as far to one end as possible, while he took the other. Crossing his knees, he got out his pipe.

As he puffed to get it lit, he said, "I'm sorry, in a way, to have to thwart your plans."

Torrie glanced over with swift resentment. If Father ever made jokes, she would have thought he was laughing at her.

"I really am," he insisted matter-of-factly. "When a person exhibits the stamina to go through with a venture as hazardous as yours, one must regret the necessity of stopping you. As a kindness to my curiosity, perhaps you'll tell me where you had planned to go? It's the one thing I couldn't figure out."

"You mean—" Torrie spoke hoarsely and had to start over again. "You mean you knew I was going to run away?"

"Oh yes. That was quite evident, to me at least. I doubt if the others suspected it."

"How—?"

"You've been far too willing." He smiled at her slightly. "It isn't your nature, Victoria. You don't want to go on this trip and yet you haven't made a murmur against it. The conclusion was obvious." His logic was more maddening than if he'd raved at her.

Torrie clenched her fists helplessly. "And you just let me go on thinking—!"

"It was the most peaceful way to accomplish our preparations," he said gravely. "But I still can't help wondering where you were intending to go."

"I was going to the hotel," she confessed glumly, "and then I was going to live with Grandpa."

This seemed to surprise him. "Did your grandfather know this?"

"He—he'd be happy to have me!" she said defensively.

"I see. He wasn't in on the plan. I'm glad. I'd have hated to think that when he took leave of us today he could have been hiding such a secret from me."

"Father," she said with desperate determination, "please let me go stay with Grandpa! I don't want to go on this fooli—this trip. I want to stay here, all my friends are here, and besides I'm old enough to make up my own mind. I'm not a child any more." She was watching feverishly for the least change in his expression, the littlest sign that he might just once see her side of things.

"I'm afraid you haven't thought out all the ramifications," he remarked in that classroom-lecture tone. "There's the matter of money. Your clothes, your activities—all of this will become increasingly costly within the next few years as you begin to attract young men. Unfortunately at present we do not have the sum in hand to supply your grandfather with the cash to meet these needs."

"I'll earn some. I'll get a—a—position—I'll be a governess or—"

"In the second place, unhappy though the thought is, your grandfather is almost eighty years old, and his life expectancy is, sadly, a limited one."

Torrie gulped that down in silence. It had never entered her head that Grandpa might die. He seemed so indestructible. Ever since she could remember, he had always looked just the same.

"In the third place," her father was going on impassively, "wise though he is—and I admire him deeply—he is not able to take an active part in your education and development. I trust you won't take offense when I say that you are not yet of a maturity to shape your life to your own best advantage. Age has little to do with the ripening process in people. Some girls of fourteen may indeed become intellectually stable, though I doubt if the emotions are ever in adult balance so early. However, you, my child, are not yet a woman, mentally or spiritually. I tell you this for your own good. Only when we recognize our limitations can we overcome them." He stood up and added, "It's quite late. We'll discuss these matters again some day when you are better able to be objective. Meanwhile, I believe we'll both do well to get some sleep. The first day of any enterprise is likely to be exhausting."

Tired—all at once too tired to argue, too tired really to care much—Torrie followed him up the stairs, her shoulders slanting, the hat tilted forward with the sorry angle of her head. At the door to her room, they stopped.

Speaking in a low voice now, her father said, "As far as I am concerned, this little encounter of ours is a private matter between us."

Torrie supposed she should have been grateful; at least Cal wouldn't find out and tease her—oh, he'd have loved to get his teeth into something like this!

As she went on slowly into the room, her father said,

"I trust I may have your promise not to leave the house tonight?"

Wearily Torrie nodded.

"There's one final consideration that I did not mention just now." And this time Father sounded almost hesitant. "In making this journey, it means a great deal to me to have our family together."

When she still did not answer, he finally closed the door. And Torrie's excursion into freedom was over.

It was a strange sight for the quiet old St. Louis street that next morning: Thomas and Caleb going through the unfamiliar procedure of yoking the three pair of stolid blinking oxen. Grandpa had brought the teams over yesterday, stupid-looking animals. He had also brought extra leather and iron to carry down on the bottom of the wagon where the spare wagon tongue was slung. "Won't be no wagon shops out there to patch you up if you break down," he warned.

The dawn twilight was hushed, the rest of the neighborhood sleeping, as Liza moved silently back and forth, carrying out the last of their belongings. The bed of the wagon was loaded so full that it was almost level with the tailgate, and some things had even been hung up under the towering round expanse of the canvas top. In the forward part of the wagon there was barely room to squeeze through to get to the seat up in front. On one side was the high mahogany bureau of drawers, the best piece of furniture they had; on the other side was a small cookstove, another of Grandpa's contributions.

When everything else was in, Torrie and her mother

carried out the mattresses and laid them over the rest of the load. Perspiring, shivering, miserable, Torrie shoved and pushed at the bulky feather ticking to arrange it on top of the sacks of flour and cornmeal and grain.

"Since you're set on goin' before grass," Grandpa had said, "you better take plenty oats for the stock. It'll make a heavy load, so watch out for soft ground."

Foolish . . . foolish . . . lugging all this across Missouri, when everybody knew that these things could be bought in Independence. Everybody else, all the sensible people, were going up the river by steamboat. But Father was so set on using this awful old box of a wagon—if it had come all the way from Ohio, he said, it should be able to make another cross-country journey. Besides the trip across the state would *test* them all.

Bitterly Torrie slammed her fists into the mattress to level it on its lumpy foundation. This—instead of riding in comfort on the decks of some elegant floating palace such as she'd seen so often tied up at the levee. It was disgusting. The one time of her life when there was ever going to be a chance to walk those shining decks and mingle with really stylish people, and instead to have to go creaking and rocking across the state in a bumpy old wagon like a shiftless bunch of poor folk.

As her mother spread blankets over the mattresses, she eyed Torrie sharply. "Your color's not so good, and I mislike that cough, so you ride back here and keep covered until the day warms up."

Warm? It wasn't ever going to get warm enough to drive off the cold loneliness that gripped Torrie, but she did as she was told, glad enough to huddle down under the blankets and be sorrowful. She wished she could just go to sleep and wake up years from now.

And yet at the last minute, when it was time to go, she sat up for one last look. The brown shingle house looked positively forsaken with its curtainless windows. The snow that still covered the yard was all chopped up by the hoofs of the oxen. The sight of Father on the big old Roman-nosed black horse would have been ludicrous if it weren't so sad. Father sat awkwardly and the horse looked miserable. He seemed aware that he was leaving forever the comfortable barn and Grandpa, who was always so kind about extra oats. And he must have guessed by now that Father was no expert rider like Grandpa.

And then, remembering that she had probably seen the old man for the last time, Torrie folded onto the lumpy mattress and wept.

Up in front, Mother and Cal had settled themselves on the seat just inside the opening in the canvas. Father seemed to be trying to get the oxen started, but nothing happened.

"Make the whip crack over their heads," suggested Mother in a troubled whisper.

"That is precisely what I am attempting to do," Father muttered almost irritably. "The confounded brutes won't move."

"I reckon you'll have to get down and lead 'em," Mother said.

"I do not intend to lead these beasts to California," Father announced grimly in hushed tones. "They are perfectly capable of moving under their own impulse. I don't want to lash the poor creatures, but—"

"Wait! I know!" Caleb interrupted eagerly. And the next instant, the quiet, slumbrous atmosphere was rent by a terrible yell. "EEEE-Yah-HAH!"

The wagon jolted forward and they were on their way.

27

APRIL

"I BELIEVE that we are entering Independence!" Father called out, and for once his calm tones seemed charged with some emotion, although Torrie, huddled in the comforter inside the wagon, wasn't sure whether he sounded excited or merely relieved.

He was walking up in front beside the teams now—he had learned that much during this long miserable month since they had left St. Louis. The oxen handled better from the ground, where they could be prodded and herded and led. Oh yes, she thought scornfully, Father could lecture people, but he couldn't talk the oxen into a thing! They had to be guided, by the rings in their noses, around the soft spots, across rushing creeks, through the mud. . . .

The endless mud! Torrents of rain had beat down on them almost since the first day of their journey. The wagon had lurched and slithered along, an inch at a time, it seemed. The "drouth of March" had turned out to be more like a flood—which just went to show how senseless poetry was!

All in all, it had been a wretched time. In several places,

the wagon had almost got stuck permanently. Their clothes had become damp clear through and never dried out. The old black horse had got untied one night and had to be hunted—they'd found him ambling along unhappily, back down the road toward St. Louis. Torrie's cough had grown worse. She just hoped they were all satisfied with the ruination they had made of things!

Not that the rest of the family was enjoying it much either—that was one small source of mean gratification. Father was so stiff from the unusual exercise that at times he could hardly hobble. Mother had remained stolid and silent as she struggled with the new strange life, the cramped quarters, and the soddening never-ending rain. After some days, they had got broken in to their duties and even accustomed to the meager meals that had to be cooked all in one pan atop the small stove, while wet wood smoked up the wagon. But being used to it didn't make it any more bearable.

Even Cal was bored after the first week, and Torrie had spent more time fighting with him than ever before in her life, forced as they were to share the same mildewing mattress, riding day after day within easy strangling reach of each other. On and on they had gone, through one little settlement after another, where the country folk stood in their doorways to gawk.

This one that they were coming into now, though, was different. The shouting and bustling noise of activity prodded Torrie's curiosity so that she finally roused and put on a shawl. Crawling forward, she lifted the piece of canvas that had been hung across just beyond the big bureau, to keep drafts out, and scrambled onto the front seat where Mother and Cal were sitting. She found that they were really in the streets of a town—a swarming market place of a town! And, as if to add a final welcome touch to the air of festivity, at that moment the sun came out weakly and Torrie's spirits rose as if a nightmare had ended.

It would have been impossible not to be excited about Independence. In her wildest imaginings, she had never expected to see such a conglomeration—wagons everywhere, crowding the streets, horsemen galloping in and out. Big freight vans with five or six teams of mules lumbered through the heavy mud, driven by bellowing skinners. And people—people of all descriptions. Every variety of dress from the sunbonnets and homespun of the backwoods to the brilliant brocaded gowns of eastern-looking ladies and the velvet and broadcloth of the men who escorted them. Soldiers, stevedores, and Indians—real Indians—wild blanketed savages with skin the color of old leather and terrible fierce dark eyes, bony faces painted red and white, just as the books described them. Torrie shuddered delicately, but down deep inside she was growing as buoyant as Cal.

They went straight through town and on to the outskirts, where a huge campground had sprung up, wagons of every description dotting the open meadows. Tents and stock were scattered all over the place, smoke rising from a hundred campfires. Thomas brought the oxen to a halt on an open patch of grass.

"I'm unhappy to say that we're a little behind my original schedule," he told them. "Nevertheless we must stay here a few days to rest the stock and purchase last-minute supplies. I wish we could see some way to hire a driver...."

It was the one difficulty that loomed the largest after

this first month. So much of the time, Father had to ride ahead on horseback, searching out ways to cross swollen streams or to get around washed-out places in the road, all the while the wagon stood still and waited. And later on, after they left the settlements, he would have to hunt game to add to their food supply. Mother could drive—she was even a little better with the whip than Father—but he said it was too hard work for a woman. And every time Cal tried, the wagon wound up stuck in the mud. So it meant that their progress had been slower than Father cared to admit, and the only solution was to hire a teamster to drive. Whenever they had talked about it, though, Father looked troubled. Wages for a man for the next six or seven months was more than they could well afford.

The smallness of their little cash became increasingly evident that night as they went over the list of necessities that they had found lacking on the trip. As Thomas had predicted, it had proven a real trial of their goods and equipment. The oxen were holding up well and the wagon had acquitted itself admirably. But there were so many things they had underestimated. Their clothing had proven distressingly inadequate. What was warm enough for the city felt thin under the buffets of chilly wind out in the open stretches of the country. The canvas top was hardly any protection at all from the cold of the nights—their blankets were so insufficient they had had to sleep close together and double up on coverlets. And there were never enough dry socks.

It was plain, too, that they would need more grain. Even though the cattle would soon be able to live off the prairie grass that would be springing up with the first sunshine, Father was convinced that they must take a supply of oats, nevertheless. Blackie would need grain and besides, he said, it would be well to have extra food—rich food—for the oxen in case of some emergency.

Furthermore, Thomas was bent on buying an extra team, which was probably going to cost dearly. And he wanted a milch cow! Of all the ridiculous ideas—Torrie could just picture herself having to go out and milk some cantankerous cow in the evening drizzle. She'd only done a little milking out at the farm, and didn't care much for it under the best conditions. But that was Father! He seemed certain that they were all going to be sickly if they didn't have fresh milk on the way.

Mother evidently felt a cow to be excessive too. In her flat disapproving manner she spoke out more emphatically than usual. "A whole herd of extra stock's going to slow us down, grass'll get scarce come end of summer, and we can't carry water for so many on the dry stretches."

A little wearily, Father smiled his tolerant smile. "I agree that it may present certain difficulties, my dear, but it is conceivable that these precautions may also save our lives, one way or another."

To think that a milk cow could save anybody's life was pretty farfetched, but now Torrie saw a curious look pass between her parents, some sort of understanding that was over her head. And that was the end of the discussion, then and there. It was also the end of any talk about hiring a driver.

That next morning, the sun came out again feebly and Liza announced that she was bound and determined to hang out the clothes and bedding to air, while she had the chance. They couldn't persuade her to go into town with them, and so, in the end, the others went without her.

Troubled somewhat by a rankling sense of guilt that she had not stayed and helped with the chores, Torrie said, "I just can't see why Mother never will let up and have a little fun."

Her father looked at her as if some private thought had touched him. "Victoria," he spoke wistfully, "it's a mistake to suppose that everyone else enjoys the same pleasures you do." She didn't exactly know what he meant, but the uneasiness of her conscience wasn't comforted by it.

As they walked through the encampment, however, her thoughts were soon distracted by the polyglot array of wagons. Some of them were small rickety home-built affairs, but most of them were new—even the wood smelled fresh and the tops were painted beautiful colors, blue, red, green. Torrie wished theirs looked half that fine. Some of them bore slogans: *Oregon, Here We Come!* and *All-out for California!* One crudely painted sign puzzled her: *54-40 or Fight!*

"What does *that* mean?" she asked her father.

"That," he said with a faint air of disgust, "represents an imaginary line on the face of the earth to which we presumably intend to stretch our boundaries, taking all of the Oregon territory without making any settlement or division with the British—who, after all, do have certain prior claims there. Actually this is one of Mr. Polk's campaign promises which has got away from him. It's an indefensible position. I'd say we'll settle for the forty-ninth parallel eventually, unless too many fools become overemotional about this slogan."

"Let's go to Oregon!" Cal suggested eagerly. "If there's going to be a war—"

"If there's a war, it will be to the south in Mexico," Thomas told him.

"But Mexico is west, where we're going, isn't it?" Torrie asked, confused. "I mean, isn't California in Mexico?"

"Technically it is under Mexican government—" Father began, when a new voice broke in on them so suddenly they all started.

"And it won't be for long, neither!" On the tailgate of one of the wagons nearby a man lounged idly, grinning at them. He was a husky fellow in sweat-stained buckskins, a flat-crowned hat tipped back on his head to let a lock of red hair sprout forward over his eyes. There was something jaunty and experienced about his whole demeanor as if all this were an old story to him. Such nonchalance Torrie thought particularly admirable in such a young man. He couldn't have been more than twenty, she calculated privately, and there was a bold humor in his smile.

"Californey's gonna be part of these-here good old United States before the snow flies this year," he told them expansively. "Once we git there, we're gonna jump in and squash that Mex government like it was a bug." He winked at Torrie, then said to her father, "Ain't that so, perfessor?"

It made her want to giggle—the word fitted Father so exactly, with his bookish manners and his glasses. He didn't smile, though, just bowed slightly to the young man and said, "If you'll excuse us, sir—" As they walked on, Thomas murmured, almost to himself, ". . . 'as fresh as is the month of May . . .' "

"What?" Cal demanded, frowning. "What did you say?"

34

"A line from Chaucer," Father explained, "aptly describing a 'lusty bachelor.'"

The word "bachelor" pricked Torrie's attention. It occurred to her that this trip might develop some entertaining aspects after all. Wherever she looked, the men outnumbered women ten to one. She pictured herself, out somewhere in the far western reaches which were so full of monstrous animals—she was trapped somewhere, up on a rock or a low tree limb, while a—a bear or something snarled beneath. And then a handsome red-headed man came along and slew the beast with a single shot from a revolving pistol. . . . Oh, beautiful one, you shouldn't be out in this dangerous land unprotected. . . .

When they reached town, the first errand was to fit Torrie with boots, and, though she had hated the idea of the clumsy heavy-soled things, once they were on she was glad enough to have them, for the streets were an oozing morass of mud. Planking had been put down in a few places across some of the worst spots, but the rest of it was ankle-deep. Cal loved it, of course; he slogged along beside her with hat tipped back on his head at just the angle of the red-headed man's hat.

"There's a Mormon!" he whispered hoarsely.

Torrie looked up to see a man ride by on horseback. Dark-skinned, almost swarthy-black, with a fiercely handsome face, he was dressed in beautiful soft black leather; his saddle was black too, mounted with silver.

"How do you know?" she whispered back, because everybody was talking about the terrible Mormons who were also making their way west not many miles north of here—a hundred thousand of them, some said.

"It's a Mormon because he looks like the Devil," Cal explained loftily. "Everybody knows that Mormons are part-Devil and some of them even have tails!"

"Caleb!" Father had heard the last of that statement. "Don't ever let me hear you speak so again!" He was really angry, as nearly furious as he ever got. "The Mormons are a religious people, neither better nor worse than any other large group, although I'd venture to say they'll get to heaven quicker than the self-righteous men who spread scandal and lies about them. You make a fool of yourself by repeating such nonsense."

As they walked on, Torrie took a small mean pleasure in staring down her nose at Cal. "I knew that wasn't a Mormon," she said. Scowling, Caleb punched her, but it was worth it. She didn't even punch back, but picked up her skirts and walked on, ignoring him completely.

Threading their way through the crowds, they passed more of the brown-faced men in strange rich clothes, speaking some foreign tongue, and Father murmured that these were probably Mexican traders up from Santa Fe. There were other exotic-looking people, too. Long-haired, bearded northwest trappers with their slurring French accents; Torrie recognized them from having seen so many on the levees in St. Louis. And lean weather-bitten old men in buckskins angled against the wall of a building or sat on a hitching rack, silent and apart from everyone else, staring up at the sky the same way Grandpa used to look when he was trying to judge planting time. It made Torrie homesick for the old man.

Farther on, they paused at an outfitter's to watch the people who had come upriver by steamboat, bargaining for their equipment. To listen to the prices that were being asked, Torrie had to admit it was just as well they weren't themselves starting out anew. It was simply horrifying—the traders were selling everything from needles to covered wagons, all of it three or four times as expensive as it would have been in St. Louis. Apparently the buyers were fairly aggrieved about it, to judge from the scraps of talk that drifted out.

"That wagon's gonna cost me my gold teeth, brother. Ain't you got a cheaper one?"

"You buy a cheaper one and you won't live to need your gold teeth—she'll fold up on you 'fore you hit the Platte."

"Well, I ain't buyin' today. Where-at's a body sleep these nights, when you don't have a white-top? They got a hotel in this skunk-water town?"

"Hotel? Mister, you got a fine sense of humor. There ain't been so much as half a bed for rent around here since the first of March. 'Course, if it was made worth my while I might let you sleep on the floor of my storeroom—"

Somebody else was complaining. "Fishhooks? What-for I need fishhooks, Mister? I got no time to fish."

"Brother, you are a greenhorn for sure. Don't you know you got to have goods to trade with the Injuns? Don't make 'em mad, brother, they'll hang your hair on their belt."

"Not mine they won't. I ain't got none."

As they walked on, Cal looked at his father, stricken with an awful thought. "We don't have any fishhooks!"

Thomas smiled faintly. "It occurs to me that the Indians must have been fishing with some sort of device for the last several centuries. I doubt that fishhooks are so vital a commodity on the trail."

At the stockyard, he stopped and studied the animals in the pens while Torrie fidgeted. The men who rode yipping and hooting around the corrals were a rough-looking bunch, and the mud and stench were shocking. Cal was in his proper element, she thought scornfully. He was going on like an expert about the merits of the cattle milling around inside, and Father was answering seriously—one would have thought the two of them knew what they were talking about!

As she waited impatiently, Torrie glanced around to notice a man walking up to the pens, the same red-headed man who had spoken to them, and again as she saw him a spurt of interest quickened inside her. There was something provocative about the daring look, the brawniness of him. . . .

He spotted them at once and strolled over with just the faintest strut in his stride. "Figgerin' on takin' a herd west along with you?" He grinned. "Good thing I come along. We Californ-eye-ans want none but the best breedin' blood in our herds." And all the while he kept glancing at Torrie in a way that made her color up and go warm inside. "I'll just lend you-all the benefit of my vast experience with critters," he told Father generously. "You ask anybody, perfessor, and they'll tell you that Luke Egan's got as fine an eye for a heifer as any man ever came out of Pike County."

He was talking loud enough to attract some of the loafers, who strolled over as if some sort of show were in store.

Father was about to move on, when the red-headed man blocked his way without exactly seeming to. "Now look here," he said in an injured tone. "You ain't gonna ask me to 'scuse you again? I 'scused you once when I was just dyin' to be sociable, but I take it unkind to have you rush off again. Least you kin do is give us the bennyfit of your name and the name of this purty gal—I reckon she's your sister—and the little tadpole here—"

At this terminology, Cal went red as raw beefsteak. Torrie was trying to suppress a smile—Father's sister, indeed!

"Shore," one of the loiterers hollered, "that's only bein' friendly."

There was quite a crowd by now hemming them in, a leering, cigar-chewing bunch—they looked like drifters or worse.

"Watch out, Luke!" one called. "That calf's gettin' ready to stomp ye!"

They were talking about Cal, who had shouldered forward, his fists doubled. Father hauled him back before he could untangle his voice and get out the retort that was obviously choking him.

"Our name happens to be Anders, sir," Thomas remarked courteously, "and we'll be much obliged if—"

"Lissen, how that man does talk!" Luke Egan looked around at them. "I *knowed* he was a perfessor first time I laid eyes on him, 'scusin' and obligin' and all."

Of course, Luke was just having a little fun with Father—who obviously was unable to see the humor of it—but Torrie thought the others were getting practically rude with their snickers. A good many of them had been drinking and they began to press closer, grinning into her face. Somebody pinched her elbow and she jerked away.

Father glanced around him and sighed slightly. "Pleasantries aside," he went on in that mild tone of his, "I'd be much obliged to you, sir, if you will assist me in testing this yoke of oxen." He indicated a pair of sleepy-eyed animals in the nearest pen.

At the deference in his tone, Luke Egan swelled with

satisfaction. Torrie winced a little. In comparison to the younger man's boldness, it was downright embarrassing to have Father be so humble. It came from being small, she supposed. He was just no match for a really big man, and she shouldn't blame him for it, she knew.

The redhead strutted up to the bars of the corral. "Well, now, the first test is to look into their faces and see if they got kind hearts and good sense," he began.

The men all guffawed and snorted.

Father took this quite seriously. "I appreciate your wanting to do such a thorough job, but I don't like to bother you with the more trifling phases of the business. Let's just concern ourselves with the supreme test—you know the one I mean."

Luke looked a little uncertain—it seemed to put him off-balance. But Father was already addressing the others. "Stand back, if you please—the rules of safety must be observed. I won't be responsible for anyone getting hurt. No, no, farther than that—this is a hazardous business. Thank you, thank you. . . ." He was motioning them away with such authority that the circle around him opened up; the men backed off, not knowing what they were avoiding. "No, indeed, we don't want any accidents—" Father had ushered Torrie and Cal away from the pens, too, leaving only Egan who stood there confused and yet not wanting to admit that he didn't know what was going on.

Free of the press of people now, Father looked back at the red-headed man. "All right, I believe it's safe to go ahead."

A little ruddy in the face, Luke said bluffly, "Well now, supposin' you tell me what all this falforal is about?"

"The test, young man." Anders looked at him expectantly. "Those oxen are going to have to cross the Great American Desert, you know. The first requisite is stamina —they must be able to stand up under the most tedious blast of hot wind. I suggest you start talking to them. . . ."

He was drowned out by a roar from the men around the corral. While they haw-hawed and hooted, Father led the way unhurriedly back toward town, followed by a wide-eyed boy and a daughter who was too dumfounded to say a word.

II

It was raining again; the steady drum of it on the canvas arching above her made Torrie feel the old desolation creeping back in. This week had been such a colorful one, she had almost become a little reconciled to the California project. The sight of so many other people getting ready to push westward had amazed her, and somehow partly justified Father's wild scheme. She was almost ready to admit that Grandpa must have been right, that there must be some strange fever to make whole families pull up roots and search out a new country with all its hazards.

Now, though, the feeble flicker of interest inside her was being drowned out by this rain, and by the thought that tomorrow they would take to the road again, only this time there wouldn't be a road—just some wheel ruts to follow, a few far-flung landmarks, and the rivers. Whenever men talked about going west, it was in terms of rivers. The Kansas, the Vermillion, the Blue, the Platte—all the travelers were basing their main calculations and hopes on the Platte. They pictured it as a highway leading westward through a long level valley where there'd be plenty of firewood, water at your doorstep every night, no hard pulling

38380

KEENE TEACHERS COLLEGE
LIBRARY

for the teams, good campsites. But sometimes Torrie thought they sounded a little too emphatic, as if they were covering up some secret fears that it might not all be as perfect as it had been painted.

Right now, she doubted it herself. With this rain beating down, she kept thinking back to that hard struggle across Missouri, the places they had barely got through, the hills that had been almost too steep for the six oxen. Of course, now there would be others around to share the hardships and trade help. Father had joined a wagon train.

All the emigrants were organizing into trains, for mutual assistance and protection against the Indians, but most of them were bound for Oregon. Father had finally found one that was for California, and that afternoon everybody had gathered around to get acquainted. Torrie hadn't thought much of the people they'd be traveling with. Some of the ladies were dressed up in finery almost as fussy as the women at the faculty teas which used to be held sometimes at home. They were the same sort, too—evidently considered themselves very highborn—and, for all that they were just wagon travelers too, they held themselves haughtily. They snubbed Liza, just the way the ladies at home had done. Torrie was beginning to understand why Mother had stopped attending those functions with Father—it was downright obnoxious the way these supercilious creatures acted. Curiously enough, Liza didn't seem so much bothered by them, out here in the middle of a campground. She looked them right in the eye, and answered up in her plain blunt way whenever there was a need to—pleasant, but not overawed. She wasn't half so uncomfortable as Torrie.

There didn't seem to be anybody Torrie's age in the train. Children, of course, and older girls—finicking young ladies with their hair piled up, and how they did hold their little fingers crooked as they drank their tea. They were simpering imitations of their mammas. On the other hand, there was an opposite element in the train, but Torrie didn't think they'd have much in common either—a coarse-mannered bunch of people who behaved crudely, the men spitting on the ground and swearing whenever they felt like it, the women laughing too loudly. The girls of that group were a bold lot, their sleazy dresses were cut much too low and their flippant talk made Liza purse her lips in disapproval.

All in all, the Anders family didn't seem to fit into the picture anywhere, but Father murmured that they were joining the train for reasons other than social ones, and remarked that the life of the trail would probably level some of the differences. He seemed reconciled to the lot, so Mother didn't make any objection, and of course Torrie couldn't. Cal had already had a fight with one of the other boys, so he was happy.

After a while, when they'd had enough small talk, one of the men, a Colonel Carroll, got up on one of the wagon boxes and made a speech. He was an imposing figure, towering tall above them, his flowing white hair gleaming in the sun as he exhorted them in a deep-chested voice. It turned out he had fought in the Seminole War, and he talked about the glories of the military life and the horrors of Indian fighting, the responsibilities of all pioneers, the need for faith in the flag and trust in God. What it boiled down to was that he said they must elect a captain to take charge of the train, since thirty-seven wagonloads of people must have a leader to guide and marshal them and settle all differences. He called for nominations.

Naturally he was the first one nominated, and he, then, very generously nominated another gentleman, a Mr. Beckwith. Somebody else nominated Luke Egan, and Torrie discovered for the first time that he would be traveling with their train. It was the only bright spot in the day, because once the election was over (the Colonel won in a walkaway, of course) the next thing they did was organize the rest of the people into work squads and Torrie got put on the dishwashing crew with the younger girls, which really did make her hate the whole lot of them. It was supposed to be the military way, and everybody said they were lucky to have a real Indian fighter to organize the train and lead them, but Torrie thought it was disgusting.

Now as she lay on her mattress in the gray of late afternoon and listened to the rain on the wagon top, she thought of St. Louis and the quiet easy life there and she could have wailed with homesickness. Just to make things completely worse, now there was a cow to milk!

With painful resignation, she hitched up onto her elbows and looked at her mother cutting potatoes into the pan of beef stew on the stove.

"I'll go and milk the cow, I guess," Torrie offered.

"You stay put. I don't want you out in that rain with your cough, besides you're too slow about it yet. I'll do it in a minute." Liza brushed a stray strand of hair away from her face and took up an onion, reduced it to chunks with a few swift strokes of the knife, and dropped it into the pan.

Torrie studied her mother curiously—instead of wearing down under the awkwardness and hardship of this past month, Liza actually seemed to be strengthening under it. Today at the elections she had held herself with more confidence than Torrie had ever remembered. In fact, her

44

whole bearing these days was—satisfied. Torrie marveled as she realized it, because there was nothing to be pleased over—the summer just starting and two thousand long hard miles yet to go into a land that wasn't even filled in on the map.

Now Liza put the lid back on the pot with a little positive clang and took down her heavy cape, picked up the lantern, and scrambled over the bedding past Torrie to get to the back of the wagon. Loosening the puckerstring and pushing aside the canvas, she stepped out into the rain without hesitation—almost with a zest—and climbed down the back steps that Grandpa had thoughtfully built onto the tailgate. Full of this new discovery about her mother, Torrie followed to watch. As she sat in the opening, with the fine mist of rain speckling her face, she wished she could figure out what was prompting this mood, so that she could borrow a little of it. To be glad to milk a cow on a rainy night—?

Liza took down the three-legged stool, settled it beside the impassive Guernsey which stood tied to the tailgate, chewing its cud as if it found nothing wrong with being rain-soaked and cold. The competent way those little spurts of milk splashed into the pail was another mystery to Torrie. It was some ancient instinct that came back to Mother apparently; it almost made Torrie jealous. Struggle as she might with the big warm teats, she could only squeeze out a few drops at a time, and she *knew* the cow resented it.

She watched, so engrossed with the milking that she didn't notice that a man had come up until he spoke to them.

"I'll do that for you," he said in a soft positive voice—it wasn't an offer, it was a settled fact.

45

Liza looked up at him as he stood out there darkly in the twilight. She started to shake her head. "Many thanks, but—"

He walked forward a step into the lantern glow, a strange lanky figure in homespun clothes that were soaked with rain. Water ran in little rivulets off the broad brim of his battered hat.

"It's what I hired on for," he said, unslinging a canvas roll from his shoulder and tossing it under the wagon. "Your mister told me to come out and make myself useful."

Liza held the lantern higher now to stare up at him, puzzled. It showed his face to be young, hard-jawed, and unsmiling. His eyes were water-clear in the flickering light and the eyebrows were blond as cornsilk. There was something about his face that made Torrie tremble, almost as the sight of those Indians had—something untamed, yet critically still.

For ten seconds, Mother took the measure of him, as she rose off the milking stool and faced him there in the rain. "I reckon you made a mistake and came to the wrong wagon."

"This is the right place," he told her in that quiet voice. "I looked your outfit over good before I asked your mister if I could hire on. He told me to tell you that him and the boy'll be along soon."

Something about the accent of his words reminded Torrie of the way Grandpa spoke, which was a back-east way of speech far different from the flat Missouri twang. It evidently made Liza wonder, too.

"Where are you from, young man?" she asked.

"Virginie."

"What's your name?"

"Jessen."

46

"What Jessen?"

He looked straight at her a minute before he said, "If you be going to ask an everlasting lot of questions, I can't travel with you." It wasn't spoken in a disrespectful way, but there was no mistaking the fact he meant it.

They stood there, taking the measure of each other, while Torrie held her breath—for some reason this man frightened her. And then they heard someone else coming, Father and Caleb. Sloshing up through the rain into the lantern light, they broke the tension.

"Well, here we all are." Thomas glanced quickly from one to the other of the silent pair that flanked the cow. "I see you've met Mr. Jessen, our driver."

"We were just introducing," Liza told him, without much warmth.

"Good. But you mustn't stand out in this downpour, my dear. I'm sure we men can handle the chores." Father sounded actually pleased to have got this odd person to work for them.

"And where'll *Mister* Jessen sleep?" Mother asked with a tartness in the word.

"Under the wagon, where else?" the young man said carelessly, as he settled the milking stool in a different position. Taking his place on it, he went to work in a way that made Mother's milking look weak. As he sent the creamy liquid streaming into the pail, he added over his shoulder, "You can call me Jess."

It was a silent supper they ate that night. Caleb was drowsy from the activities of the day; he'd run himself almost to exhaustion. The others were far from sleepy, however, as they sat around the stove, eating the savory stew without conversation. It was as if another presence were among them, although the stranger had refused to come in to eat his supper. Taking the plate Liza had fixed for him, he had ducked underneath with it, and that was the last they'd heard of him.

Out of the uneasy quiet Thomas spoke in a hushed voice. "Well, the young man claims he's been sleeping out all the way across country ever since February. Presumably he's —accustomed to it."

Nobody commented on that.

It made Torrie squirm inside just to think of the little runnels of water that were coursing along the ground down there, even if the wagon was some small protection against the rain itself.

After a while, Mother muttered unhappily, "I thought we decided we couldn't afford a driver."

"True, we did." Father nodded. "Today, however, I changed my mind—or rather the young man made me a proposal which I thought it possible to accept."

"What proposal?" she asked.

"That," said Father reluctantly, "is something I'm not at liberty to reveal. Part of our arrangement involves privacy."

"You mean it's a secret?" Caleb roused up blinking.

"Let's say a matter between Jess and me." And Father's tone allowed no further question.

But there was no doubt that, after the light was put out and they settled themselves under the blankets, the unspoken mystery hung over them, thicker than ever, and when Torrie finally did go to sleep, she dreamed that a strange silent young man was driving them over a terrible, dangerous road. She dreamed that all their lives were in his hands.

MAY

THAT NEXT morning, as if to make Torrie ashamed of last night's doldrums, the day turned out blazing bright, with cloudless crystalline sky—the first real day of spring. Standing out back, while the men yoked the oxen, she let the sun soak into her with new thankfulness. At home, she had never thought much about the sun, but out here on the edge of the prairies it was welcome as a miracle.

Even the new driver seemed less disturbing in the morning light. He had hung his hat on the brake handle of the wagon to dry and went about his work with his blond hair loose to the fresh breeze that had sprung up. It made him look more boyish than Torrie had thought, although he handled the stock with all the authority of an old hand.

She couldn't help being puzzled by him. He had hardly spoken a word and seemed to pay fixed attention to what he was doing until, once in a while, he would glance up, and then the deep-set eyes almost scorched her, as if he were smoldering with some odd resentment. It wasn't really personal—and yet it was. When he looked at her, Torrie was vividly aware of it.

49

A little flustered, she hustled about, helping her mother finish packing. The washpan had to be tied down to the outside of the wagon, the milk pail and stool fastened in place. Caleb brought the cow in from the spot where she had been staked out for the night and they milked her and tethered her to the tailgate. The extra pair of oxen which Thomas had bought would be driven with the rest of the herd of loose stock of the train. Finally Father saddled old Blackie and swung up. Caleb and Mother were already on the front seat of the wagon, while Torrie lingered in the sunlight, reluctant to climb into the old schooner and set out upon the trail. And, suddenly, they realized that Jess had disappeared.

Thomas looked around with slight concern—the other wagons had started rolling out some minutes earlier, waving as they went past with just a touch of superiority at having got on their way first.

"Well now," said Liza, peering out the front flap of the wagon, "we can't wait around—"

"One moment, my dear." Father stared past the wagon. "Here he comes now." And then he added, with a sort of inward amusement, ". . . 'As lean was his poor horse as is a rake.' "

For Jess was leading a horse across the meadow, a gaunt sorrel mare, each rib standing out on her flanks, the hip-bones jutting up sharp enough to stretch the skin of her hollow haunches.

"Had her staked out down a piece from here," Jess explained to Thomas, as he tied the mare to the tailgate.

"I didn't know you had a mount," Father said. "You should have brought her over earlier when I was graining Blackie."

"You never promised grain for my mare," said Jess almost truculently. "She'll make out on grass. It's her nature to be some thin." Then glancing over his shoulder at Torrie who had paused to stare at the long-legged animal, he added, "It ain't her nature to be kindly, though. You'd best keep clear of her south end, little girl."

And with that, as coolly as if he hadn't just tossed off an utterly shocking insult, he picked up the bullwhip, whooped to the oxen and they started so readily that Torrie, for all her indignation, had to jump lively to get up onto the tailgate. Making a big semicircle, they headed out westward, away from the last outpost of the civilized world.

Those first days on the trail, the prairie came to life around them. Whereas traces of green had just begun to show far down in the roots of the dry stubble of the campground in Independence, out here under the sun the grass was shooting up thick and choice. Even in the short evening grazing time, the cattle began to pick up weight on it—Torrie remembered how Grandpa used to say the first growth was always the richest.

Flowers too were breaking out in the young clean yellows and pinks of springtime, all along the rolling slopes through which the train moved. At first, the country was a good deal like Missouri, with rocky outcroppings, patches of woodland, little freshets. And then they left the trees behind and found themselves at sea upon an undulating grassland that stretched ahead as far as they could see. The dome of the sky was like a brilliant cloudless globe of blue china above them. A wonderful spring smell rose in the warm air, better than new hay or flowers or wet earth, but made up of all three.

And not the least of the beauty of it was that long line

of white-topped wagons rolling on ahead. There was something fine about them—Torrie understood a little what Grandpa had meant when she saw the train breasting the swell of the green land. There were other trains ahead, and behind them too. On the crests of the low hills, when she looked either forward or back, she could see them scattered irregularly, from one end of the land to the other. Most of them were emigrants, although occasionally a long line of freighters would pull slowly past, beating a new wheel-track of its own as it forged ahead, urged on by roaring bullwhackers. To one huge van, Torrie saw ten yoke of oxen hitched.

And then, near the end of the first week, they reached the junction where the trail divided—one arm reaching off straight west, which the freighters were all taking, the trail to Sante Fe. The other veered north—the route that both the California and Oregon trains would follow until some far-distant point when it would branch again. As Jess headed the teams up the right-hand track, they passed a sign that made even the most skeptical person quicken inside:

ROAD TO OREGON

II

As long as the weather was fine and cool, the prairie was pleasant enough, though endlessly monotonous, and life on the trail was not too difficult. But when, in the latter days of May, the breeze swung up from the south and the heat began to mount, the cloudless sky and shadeless plains began to be a matter of irritation, then outright dread. The strangeness of this vast country grew less intriguing and more hostile as the endless rise and fall of the land began to shimmer with heat. It was then that the trains drew apart, some pushing on at a faster pace, others growing discouraged and turning back.

Oddly enough, the nights were still cool—almost cold. The stars came out brilliantly and the blankets had to be pulled up. But each morning, with the first flood of daylight across the land, the chill would vanish, and by noon the sun would be harsh as a fire beating down on them. The only way to get out of it was to stay in the wagon, but that was almost worse. Under the canvas top, the air got hot enough to bake bread.

For a while, Torrie tried sitting on the front seat, but the dusty haze kicked up by the wagons ahead was thick enough to chew. She sometimes wondered how Jess could stand it. Out there in the worst of the sun and dust, he walked tirelessly beside the teams, watching for any animal to slack its share of the pull, heading them around the roughest spots of the trail, just with a quick word of command. He hardly ever touched them with the whip, as they had come to respond to his voice.

Torrie wasn't sure just how he did manage them—he seldom spoke loud enough for her to hear. Now Luke Egan was a man with a fine voice! You could hear him all over the train, and when he yelled an order at his driver or the oxen, it was in colorful masculine language that made Father wince and Mother frown, but which drew a little secret smile from Torrie sometimes. It was so manly!

Luke was a fine-looking sight, too, as he rode his big buckskin up and down the train. It was a spirited animal and gave him a lot of trouble, but he sat it beautifully, that hat always tipped back on his head, the carrot-colored hair bursting out the front of it. Oh, he was a little bit bully, Torrie knew that! But she couldn't help being tantalized by him, just as all the other girls were. He was considered the "catch" of the whole wagon train. So young to have an outfit of his own. No hawk-eyed mother to shoo the girls away, either. So they made an outrageous play for him, and Torrie herself took whatever opportunity presented itself to smile. She could see that he was interested in her in some different way than his flippant camaraderie with the others. When he met her eyes and smiled back at her or tipped his hat with a little flourish, there was something unreadable in his look. Torrie was vastly flattered.

Of course Mother and Father took a very dim view of her being nice to Luke. It was as if they didn't want her ever to associate with men at all—just as it had been at home. In fact, if anything, this trip was making them both stubborner. Mother's face was getting more determined all the time, her freckles standing out bold now that her face was tanning from the sun. She had lost a little weight, but actually it made her look better. And Father was looking quite different, what with having grown a small black beard. He was even beginning to handle the horse with more authority, although the strenuous exercise still left him terribly tired, especially now that he had taken it upon himself to scout for water every day. Always worrying! Torrie thought irritably.

Of course it was true, the streams were getting farther apart as they plodded on deeper into the heart of the prairie. But she couldn't see why he had to be so strict about their drinking water. Every time they left one creek and headed out over a dry stretch for the next one, he would insist that they all fill their jugs, and he and Jess would fill the big casks lashed to the outside of the wagon—these were for the oxen and couldn't be touched until Father had ridden ahead and made sure they would come to another watering spot by sundown. It seemed just maddening. Last month they were all practically drowning in rain, and now, when the jugs were empty, they couldn't even have a sip of the oxen's water. Nobody else worried whether there was water ahead.

And to think that they could have all been back in St. Louis, where a drink is something you took for granted!

Miserably Torrie squirmed at the thought. It was the hottest day yet, and she had gone back to lie on the mattresses in the rear of the wagon, near the opening, where she could get a little air without quite so much dust.

"I wish we'd get to this Platte River," she groaned. "I thought it was right near Independence, the way everybody was going on about it."

"Some folks like to make things sound easy." Liza went on with her mending. She was darning a pair of Cal's linsey-woolsey pants. He seemed to tear some part of himself every time he moved, the horrid little monster. Torrie wondered if he had any water left. She was just about to hunt for his jug, when the boy swung up into the wagon over the tailgate. He looked red-faced and irritated and hot. Beckoning her to follow him up front where they weren't right under Mother's nose, he said in a dire whisper, "That Jess is—listen, I'll bet he's a convict or an escaped prisoner or he jumped off a ship or killed somebody or something!"

"Why?" demanded Torrie in equally muted tones. "What makes you think so?"

"Because he won't tell his name," Cal said grimly.

"There must be something turrible bad about anybody that won't give their name. I hinted and I hinted, but he wouldn't even hardly talk to me. So I finally asked him. I was out there helping him drive just now, and I told him we needed to know how to spell his first name on account of we were keeping a journal, like Colonel Carroll."

Privately Torrie marveled at what an excellent excuse he'd thought up—everybody knew the Colonel was keeping a careful record of each day's travel, what the temperatures had been, what animals they'd seen and birds and all that. That's why he never had time to help with the regular chores of camp—he was making entries every evening.

"What did Jess say when you told him that?" she demanded, prickling with curiosity.

"He got mad! He got awful mad!" Cal chewed his lip cruelly. "But I'll get even with him for it, you wait!"

"For what?"

"What he said. He said, 'The cow just bawled, why don't you go make a note in your journal about it?' That's what he said."

"That's all?"

"Well, it was the mean way he said it!" Irritably, Cal pounded her on the shoulder with his fist. "You're so dumb!"

"*You're* dumb, you little beast!" Torrie snatched at him and missed. "You ought to be *tied* out back alongside the cow, that's what I think. With a ring in your nose!" And when Liza looked around at them, frowning, Torrie explained with suppressed fury, "He hit me!"

Disgusted, Mother shook her head a little, but before she could scold, they heard a commotion outside, everybody shouting and talking, women crying—it sounded as if they'd caught up with a convention or something. The wagon had stopped, which meant the whole train had come to a halt. All three of them were distracted from their squabble, and Cal lost no time in scrambling out the rear, with Torrie close behind.

The scene which sprawled before them was tragic. Another group of emigrants was milling around, helter-skelter, staring at their wagons, which were partly burned, the canvas tops slashed in places. Worst of all was the pitiful handful of oxen, wild-eyed and bleeding from wounds in their shoulders or hindquarters. They churned and bellowed, while the women wept and the men stood around disheartened. Everybody looked scared to death.

Pawnee ... Pawnee ... the word came down the line of their own train, as the other people told their story to Colonel Carroll. The Pawnees had attacked them at daybreak this morning. They admitted that the evening before they hadn't made a very neat corral—that is, the circle which each train formed with the wagons every night, where they kept their herd of stock for protection. They hadn't posted a guard, either, and when the Indians had come screeching down upon them in the early dawn, the cattle had bolted. The men had managed to drive off the attack after some shooting back and forth, but the Indians had taken most of the oxen with them except for these few miserable animals.

By the time they had finished their sorry tale, everyone in the Colonel's train was looking over their shoulders at the empty land stretching away from them on all sides. It was easy to imagine savages just over the next rise of hills.

Them Injuns ... silent as serpents ... clever as cats. ...

57

The words rushed along the halted train, and every driver was ready to crack the whip when the Colonel gave the signal with his hand which was his army sign, meaning "Forward!"

Torrie and Cal climbed back up onto the tailgate of the wagon. He was sweating with envy of a boy in the other train who was flourishing a real Pawnee arrow. As the train jolted forward again and they moved slowly on past the luckless party, the poor dismayed people stood blinking.

"What are we going to do?" one woman wailed.

And another called out furiously, "You got extry oxen. Least you could do is give 'em to us!"

Liza went back to her work with a sigh. "Poor fools, they might as well expect us to give 'em our extra clothes and victuals, too. Can't see why the shiftless ones that don't bother to guard their own property always think providence is going to take care of 'em." She muttered on to herself while Torrie leaned back on the mattresses and wondered how long it takes a person to die of thirst.

Of course after the first flurry of fear, the Indian scare died down along the train. There was a tremendous lot of talk about Indian tortures and how they lifted a scalp, but nobody really seemed to think it could happen here, to this train. In broad daylight? Dawn is the time when the Indians always attack, as everybody knows. Nevertheless, they did send Luke Egan out ahead to scout for "Indian sign," although nobody seemed very positive just what "Indian sign" was.

Torrie wasn't particularly frightened, but it did give a person pause to think, because they were alone now. Most of the trains had finally pushed ahead of theirs, inasmuch as the Colonel insisted on stopping so early every day. A good many of the other men, including Father, objected to it, but the Colonel always said his wife was feeling frail and couldn't travel any more that day. She was too frail to help with the chores, too, and so were Mrs. Beckwith and a number of the other ladies of that group. They had weak spells whenever it came time to cook, but once supper was ready, Torrie noticed they all had appetites as healthy as any man's.

The same was true when it came to dishwashing; the younger ladies of those fine families were all out collecting "botanical specimens"—which meant they were picking flowers. And the bolder girls from the other side of camp would be dallying and gossiping, switching their hips at the young bucks, especially Luke Egan. Torrie, elbow-deep in soapsuds, was thoroughly galled—for no matter how unequal things got, Mother would never have let her shirk her chores.

Cal had figured things out from the beginning. Torrie could say that for him. He saw that none of the other boys were going to worry much about firewood, so he usually skipped out the minute the train stopped to make camp. It always made Liza's lips tighten, but she wouldn't scold him. Cal was Father's problem, she made it plain, all the while she concentrated even harder on seeing that Torrie was conscientious.

So, as she soaped off the pots and pans, Torrie would fume and glare at the lazy hussies who lolled around the fire where the men were usually singing songs—"Old Dan Tucker" and some of these new minstrel tunes, like "Skip to My Lou." Luke Egan's strong tenor carried out lustily over the voices of the other men, and you'd think he was really enjoying himself with all the fiddle-faddle, when actually he was probably tired to death of those girls and their inane talk. And Torrie would go over whole beautiful little speeches that might some day be used to engage his admiration so that he'd forget—or forgive—the fact that she was, essentially, in all truth, rather—plain.

That unhappy realization persisted in dogging her these long idle days. She was thinking about it now, as the old wagon creaked and bumped along in the heat. And just as she was wondering if lack of water was going to contribute to her scrawny looks and even leave her permanently wrinkled, Father came riding back with the news that water was ahead—they'd reach a new stream by tonight. Torrie and Cal scrambled down the tailgate and rushed around to the casks—the water was warm and stale, but they gulped it gratefully.

Meanwhile, Mother told about the people who'd been attacked by Indians. Father looked grave as he listened to the news. He hadn't passed the damaged train on his way in search of a stream because he'd veered away from the trail to look for game as he rode. Several of the men had shot birds and once they'd got an antelope, but that was all the fresh meat they had tasted since they'd left Independence, mostly because the rest of the men didn't hunt very hard, and Father himself wasn't very good with the rifle yet. But he always tried, roving far out across the prairies, and now it startled them all to think that he might have stumbled onto the Pawnee war party while he was alone. At least everyone was dismayed except Father himself.

He said, "That was a possibility I foresaw some days ago —it has seemed necessary to risk it. However, this actual evidence of the red man's presence is disturbing. We ourselves do not always take enough trouble to shape a trim corral. I believe I must speak to the Colonel—" But before he could say what was on his mind, they were interrupted by a cry, a halloo from somewhere far out across the grassland.

"Buf-fa-lo . . . Buf-fa-lo!"

A minute later, Luke Egan came pounding in on the buckskin horse. "Buffalo!" he was shouting. "A whole herd of 'em, right over the next ridge!"

In twenty minutes, every man of the train was on his horse, flourishing some sort of gun, ready to get in the chase. Everyone except Father. He even went so far as to ride out in front of the Colonel, and then and there, before them all, said that some sort of guard should be left with the train.

"Can you really be so unconcerned about the Indians," he demanded, "that you'll leave the train unprotected except for the drivers—who would have their hands full, heaven knows, trying to form a corral if the Pawnees should attack? Certainly some of you would do better to stay here and let the others attend the hunting!"

Everybody laughed, and then, with a little mockery, they badgered him to brace up and not be scare-minded, to come along with them. And off they went.

Torrie felt absolutely degraded. She was as humiliated as Cal, to think that, at very first sight of buffalo, their own father was the only one who didn't at least try for a kill. Indians—out here in the afternoon sunlight? It was just ridiculous.

As she and Cal scrunched down disconsolately in the back opening of the wagon, they watched their father gloomily as he rode down along the part of the train that was strung out behind them. He was trying to get the wagons to stay in line. But the first half of the train was raising a choking cloud of dust, and the people behind were fanning out across the prairie to get away from it; each wagon was picking its own way, which was easy to do now that the ground was so dry.

Torrie sighed unhappily—Father would always be a schoolteacher, making people be neat and do everything just so. Her indignation flickered out to ashes, leaving her just feeling sorry for him. By tonight, he'd be the most looked-down-on man in the wagon train. Furthermore, the people back there weren't paying any attention to him, they were straying farther and farther from the trail, and every now and again one of the wagons would go completely out of sight behind some swell of the land. For a while, Father crisscrossed back and forth between them, but finally he came riding back, disheartened.

The only thing that could be said for Father was that he did know there was water ahead and managed to talk the Colonel's "ailing" wife into going on until they got to it. It was almost sundown when they finally reached the river and the men still hadn't returned from the hunt. Strangely enough, Father gave a few quiet instructions to the drivers and got the wagons marshaled into a better corral than they usually managed with the whole bunch of men racketing about and shouting directions. Torrie had to admit that it was astonishing how easily Father organized that circle, leaving just enough room for the wagons that were still straggling in tardily after roaming so wide of the trail. In fact, one of them—the Duncan family—didn't come in at all.

Mr. Duncan was doing his own driving and so hadn't

been able to go on the hunt. Now, when they didn't show up, no one was particularly worried except Father. The other families just shrugged and said, oh, they'd be along soon.

Thomas rode up to the top of the last ridge, but couldn't see sight of them. Coming back to their own wagon, he got out the Colt revolver. Shaking his head, he said, "Duncan cursed me most soundly when I tried to tell him it was dangerous not to stay with the others."

Liza watched him load the gun anxiously. "It's not your job to go looking for them."

"In this undertaking, it is necessary to consider that we are all members of each other," Thomas said sternly. "The safety of all depends on the safety of each. I shall make this clear to the Colonel when he returns."

Torrie sighed. They were really going to be unpopular with the whole train if Father persisted in being such a fussbudget. "But Indians don't ever attack in the daytime, do they?" she asked.

Thomas looked at her strangely. "Why do you suppose I stayed with the train this afternoon, Victoria, instead of raging off in search of the shaggy monster, like a Homeric hero?"

Torrie fell silent, but Caleb spoke up naïvely. "Because you're not a very good shot?"

Father's lips tightened slightly, but as usual he answered Cal patiently. "Allow me credit for a little more intelligence than that, my son. The accuracy of my marksmanship would be and shall be improved with practice, but I trust I shall never become intoxicated with the lust of the kill to the point where all else is neglected. To quote the advice of a very sage philosopher, it is dangerous to indulge in

63

frivolities while an enemy may lurk in wait for just such an unguarded moment."

"Did Chaucer say *that?*" Torrie wondered weakly.

"No," her father said, "it was another pilgrim—your grandfather. I believe his exact words were, 'When there's Injuns about, don't get drunk.'"

As he went off looking for the Duncans, a small figure mismatched with the big horse, Mother watched him go across the lengthening sun-and-shadow patterns that the sunset was making. Torrie felt a certain sympathy for her, but when Liza turned and caught a glimpse of it, her disapproval came under quick control and she only said, "Come along, there's work to be done."

Tonight, for some reason, the other women came forward too, and if they didn't exactly work, they puttered around the fire as if they needed to keep close together. They were anxious, now, about their men. Casting troubled glances along the back trail, they set up a fruitless chitchat to cover their growing apprehension and even dabbed at the cooking. It was the first time Torrie had ever seen Mrs. Beckwith peel a potato. The Colonel's wife still wouldn't touch any part of the chores—she was a cold silver-haired woman with pale smooth hands that looked as if she never used them. It almost made Torrie proud of the way Mother's blunt competent fingers went about the work, got a job done and done right.

All work stopped short, though, when they saw the men trooping home over the hills. Even before they reached camp, it was plain they'd got a buffalo. Big dripping chunks of meat were tied to each one's saddle, and the Colonel carried the hide, done up in a huge hairy bundle. Luke Egan was holding aloft the beast's grotesque head

64

—horns and all—ugly as a fiend out of Satan's nether world. Everybody clustered around him as he swung down off the buckskin, marvelously stained with dirt and blood.

He nodded to their questions. "I shot it."

The Colonel seemed put out by that statement. "We all engineered the kill," he boomed impressively. "We pursued the wily beasts for miles until my strategy was applied, of circling around to intercept their path of flight. . . ."

He broke off short as Liza thrust her way through the crowd and walked up to confront him. Torrie gasped, to see Mother interrupt anyone, much less the Colonel himself, and everybody else fell silent with shock too. Planting herself firmly, her fists dug into her ample hips, Liza said, "And while you were out chasing a bunch of animals, your train was going to pieces. Some of your knucklehead friends went rambling off in spite of everything we could do to stop 'em and now they're lost out yonder, and my man's gone alone to find 'em. So I figger you better get right back on that horse and go out and help him, long as you're supposed to be captain of this train."

Her words transfixed the lot of them. Not only had most of them never heard Liza say a word before, but nobody certainly had suspected that such a rage could smolder inside her—it had burst into a small bright flame when she'd said "my man."

A shiver of excitement went over Torrie. It was as if she had never really seen her mother before—as if this were someone new, a strange woman with fierce feelings. A woman who loved Father!

After a certain amount of huffing and muttering, the men did mount up again unwillingly and rode off to look for the missing party. Luke Egan didn't go with them—

65

he announced that somebody had better stay with the women to protect them, only he made it sound bold and courageous, instead of apprehensive. It was all in a person's manner and air, Torrie thought. The way Luke began to hustle them around was most marvelous—he even got the women to working, telling them how to put the meat on to roast, then set the girls to watch for any movement out across the land where dusk was settling in.

"Let's see if those purty eyes of yours are sharp, too," he told them, grinning.

But when he shouted for somebody to take care of his horse, his own driver wasn't around, and the other men didn't scurry to his orders like the females. The Colonel's hired hands glowered and turned away. Mr. Beckwith's teamster delivered a string of profanity that made Torrie blush.

Luke was beginning to get riled. "I got important duties, and I'm in charge here 'til the Colonel gets back!" he roared. "Jessen, pull the saddle off my horse!"

Torrie held her breath, expecting an explosion, for there was already some tension between these two. Whenever they broke the corral there was likely to be a clash. Luke was never one to want to take a back place in the train, and once Jess had to cut their own team in front of Luke's when it came the Anderses' turn to go ahead. It was one of the rules of the trail, rotating places each day so that nobody got too much dust, and Jess was adept about establishing their rightful place in line. But it made Luke furious. And now Torrie expected open trouble.

But Jess walked over to the buckskin without a word and began to loosen the cinch.

Egan grinned broader than usual. "Glad to see at least one person around here has got the proper respect."

66

As Jess hauled the handsome tooled-leather saddle from the foam-flecked back of the buckskin, he glanced over his shoulder. "I got plenty of respect for your horse," he drawled, and, with a careless gesture, dumped the saddle upside down in the pile of fresh ox dung.

Speechless with outrage, Luke strode forward—Jess waited for him, hands loose at his sides. Luke was so much heavier than the yellow-haired Virginian that Torrie feared wildly, for a moment, that he might kill Jess. Glancing around desperately, she saw something to divert them.

"Here they come!" she cried frantically. "Look—look!"

And indeed, across the prairie came a slow-moving procession. All other thoughts were forgotten as they rushed to meet the rescuers, who brought the frightened family in, limping. The top of Duncan's wagon was tattered and burned, and he was driving only two yoke of oxen. The Pawnees had caught them, shot burning arrows at their canvas, killed two of the oxen. Mr. Duncan had driven them off with his pistol, but he was unnerved and Mrs. Duncan was in tears. Their terror seemed to have touched even the brashest of the men, who now dismounted in silence.

When they'd all gathered around the fire, the Colonel spoke uneasily, but still trying to sound hearty and authoritative. "Now, then, Anders, you made some rather blunt charges out there on the trail in the heat of emotion. Do you wish to repeat them or shall we just forget this incident?"

Father confronted him with a touch of asperity showing through his even temper. "I seldom speak from undue emotion, sir," he said, "and we shall certainly none of us profit by forgetting this misfortune. I'll gladly repeat that I feel this train to be suffering from lack of leadership. Furthermore, the communal effort is slovenly—there has not been a proper sharing of duties. Even the basic rules of sanitation have become so ignored we are all likely to suffer illness if it continues. I see garbage and offal on the ground—there's been no effort to dig a slop pit for the last five evenings. The herd is not properly tended—unless my driver and I watch the stock, it is allowed to wander and scatter these evenings. I believe the two of us have brought them into the corral every night for the past week, un-aided."

"And what's more," broke in Luke Egan loudly, "we're movin' too consarned slow. We're stoppin' when the sun's three-o'clock high, we're never gonna get to Californey that way. I say this train needs a new leader, all right, some-body that'll put some stuffin' into it. I'm tired of bein' shoved back to the rear whiles the Colonel here always jumps into the leadoff spot. And I don't like bein' told I didn't shoot me a buffalo when I went and did. It was my shot brought the critter down and I near caught the Colonel hikin' off with the best part of the meat. If that's how this train's gonna be run, I'm organizin' a new train right here'n now. Anybody wants to come with me can step over to this side of the fire!"

It all happened so fast, Torrie hardly could realize it. Their train was splitting up! As they argued and milled around choosing sides and calling names, she looked for Father, but he and Mother were nowhere in sight; he'd disappeared while Luke was speechifying. She went back to their wagon and found them, with Jess, standing in sober conference.

"It's a serious thing." Father was shaking his head. "We're in a bad spot, I'm afraid. If Egan hadn't made a

68

personal issue out of this, we might have had some orderly change. Now, with the group dividing in two hostile parts, neither half is going to have sufficient strength to stand off a serious Indian attack."

"Not only that, but neither one of those men is worth shucks," Liza stated flatly.

"I'm afraid you're right," Father agreed, while Torrie wondered how they could be so blind. Because obviously Luke was the man to get things done, without all the high-falutin army rigamarole that the Colonel liked to put on. But nobody was going to ask her opinion.

Instead, Father looked at Jess. "Do you have any suggestions as to which party we should join?"

The Virginian looked down at the hat in his hands, rolled the brim intently as he studied the question.

Father added, "Egan will travel faster, he'll keep discipline for the pure joy of giving orders, whether he's fair about it or not."

Jess nodded. "He'll bull his way through. Colonel could get us all killed." Then he eyed Thomas calmly. "Only right for me to tell you, though, that if we go with the new train, sooner or later Luke and me are going to fight." And then, for some reason, he glanced at Torrie.

JUNE

THE PLATTE—! This Platte River that everyone had been looking forward to reaching, as if it were the highway to heaven—it was the worst excuse for a river that Torrie had ever seen. A mile-wide muddy bottom through which the shallow water meandered, water so thick it had to be let stand overnight before it could be drunk. Worse than Missouri River water, which they said would grow vegetables right in your glass.

Furthermore, the whole floor of the mud flat was clotted with willows and underbrush. Even though the trail itself was on higher dry ground, the mosquitoes and gnats were all over everybody all the time—buzzing in your ears, getting in your eyes and mouth. Small hostilities were abuzz too.

Almost everybody resented the way Luke made them stick to their chores. Just as Father had predicted, he seemed to relish giving orders. He didn't even let Cal sneak off, but kept the boy on the hop, collecting dry buffalo dung. Most of the time, that was all they could find to

70

make a fire with; what wood wasn't too green to burn had already been used up by the trains ahead of them. It was a task that made Cal almost tearful with rage, though Torrie privately thought it served him right for dodging his duties the first part of the trip.

Mother and Father had always been ready to work hard, so it wasn't easy for Luke to show his authority over them, and, besides, Thomas took no nonsense from him. Liza was willing and able to give him the edge of her tongue any time he started to strut around her. Torrie had to admit that Luke did strut, but she justified it as a part of his personality—a sort of natural pride in himself.

He certainly was full of spirit, she thought. When a rider came through from St. Louis, heading west, and brought a week-old newspaper telling that war had been declared with Mexico, Luke made a brilliant loud speech about what he was going to do with the Mexicans when they got to California, and how he wished he were down there with old Zach Taylor right this minute, sticking a bayonet into Santa Ana's guerrillas. He went on about it until somebody's voice spoke out sourly from the group of men crowded around, and invited Luke to go ahead if he wanted to—they could spare him. For some reason that quieted him down.

But the rudeness of it irked Torrie. After all, it was natural for a man to get excited and make a few exaggerations about such matters as war. And then, without knowing quite why, she'd looked around to see where Jess was. He hadn't even come over to join the rest of them, clustering around the newspaper; instead, he was fiddling with the oxen's hoofs, checking for signs of soreness. As usual, anything to give him an excuse to hang apart from them.

Luke was hardest of all on Jess, which could be expected after the way they had clashed all along the trail. But sometimes Torrie didn't think it was quite fair, the way he always gave the Virginian the meanest jobs—digging the slop pit and, worse yet, carrying the water.

That was the detail the men hated the most. These warm evenings, it meant trip after trip to the river. Once away from the campfire where the smoke provided at least a little protection, the mosquitoes swarmed in, especially in the underbrush where there was no air stirring. It was possible to fight them off to some extent going in, but coming back with a bucket of water in each hand, a man was at their mercy. There were times when Jess would bring the wash water that Torrie felt downright grieved at the sight of him, soaked with perspiration and covered with bites. He never let her pity him long, though. He'd squelch her with one of those mocking remarks, as if he were talking to a child.

"I'd rather be mosquito-bit than moonstruck," he commented once. And it took Torrie a while to convince herself that he had actually make a personal remark that could only be insulting, whatever it meant! And she'd got even more outraged when it dawned on her that he might be referring to her friendship with Luke!

As if it were any of his business that Luke showed her a good deal of attention. Everybody—just everybody—seemed bent on running her life for her, Torrie reflected bitterly. A dogged rebellion rose inside her, and she silently defended Luke against them all.

Even if he was a little overbearing, the work was getting shared these days, and besides, underneath it all, he was really very kind. He'd taken her off the dishwashing brigade that first night after the train split up. He said it was children's work, which it was. Instead, he gave her the best assignment in camp—milking his own two cows for him. He had brought along, with his beef cattle, two good Jerseys to start a dairy herd in California, he said.

It had made Mother darken up, and they'd almost had a fight over it, with Torrie explaining that it was proper work, and Luke had every right to ask her to do it since the milk was going to be shared by other people in the train.

"It's hardly a donation," Father had remarked dryly. "He's collecting from everyone who wants his cows' milk —taking payment in lard or salt pork."

"Well, why shouldn't he?" stormed Torrie. "They're his cows!"

"The point is—" Liza began, then turned to Thomas, shaking her head as if the whole business was too much for her.

"The point is," he said, "that our daughter desires to milk Mr. Egan's cows so I suppose we may as well permit it. However, Victoria," he eyed her whimsically, "I trust you will remember the fate of Chauntecleer's young feminine friend: So full of torment and fury was she over the poor cock, that she

> Wilfully into the fire did start,
> And burned herself to death with steadfast heart.

It always seemed a great waste, to me," he added.

For some reason, both Jess's remark and Father's words kept rankling inside Torrie those next weeks as she went about milking the two cows every morning and night. Almost always, Luke would stroll over to watch her, smiling down with that strange satisfied look in his eyes—

sometimes she even wondered if it really was a flattering look. It seemed to Torrie that he might be enjoying himself a little at her expense too, watching her bend to his work. But then she always reminded herself that the other girls were green with jealousy and, besides, that grin was just Luke's natural way—it was part of his charm. She tried not to let these little doubts take hold.

She was gratified to see that some of her carefully rehearsed little bits of gaiety were pleasing him, at least he laughed quite a good deal when they talked together in the evenings. But then, just as they'd be getting quite friendly, Torrie would get the feeling that they were being watched. Sure enough, if she looked around, there would be Jess, just going by, coming back from the river or going out to bring in the herd—he always seemed unaware that he was anywhere near them, but it happened too often to be a coincidence. And once, when he did chance to glance over at Torrie, there was a gleam in his look, sharp as a knife. She hardly knew what it meant—it couldn't be what it seemed, a sort of warning to her.

Luke was beginning to notice, too, how Jess managed to be around so often, and one night his eyes narrowed suspiciously.

"What's that boy's game?" he murmured in a low voice, as they watched Jess lug the heavy buckets of water to the campfire, then head back to the river for more. "He didn't need to take no roundabout way past my wagon." Suspiciously, he frowned down at Torrie. "You wouldn't know, would you?"

She couldn't help laughing. It occurred to her that Luke was even a little jealous. Without weighing the consequences, she answered, "Nobody knows what Mr. Jessen thinks. He's the most mysterious, provoking man I ever met."

For some reason, Luke scowled darker at this. "Jessen? There's nothing so wonderful about that ox driver. He's a surly cuss."

"Who said 'wonderful'?" she demanded.

"You did. Any time a girl gets that dreamy look"—he snickered—"think I don't know what it means?"

Torrie was genuinely amazed—he was trying to tell her that she seemed to have a *liking* for Jess. "Mr. Jessen," she retorted, "is a rude unfriendly hardheaded man, and—"

"Well, well," Luke said softly, "if he's all that bad we better punish him some, hadn't we? Hey, you, Jessen, come here!" Because Jess was back from the river with another load of water. When Luke called, he set the buckets down and came over.

There was a long brush scratch on one cheek and the pale hair was plastered to his forehead. For all his leanness, he had a tempered look, taut as a coiled steel spring, and in his eyes was such a steady danger that Torrie quaked inwardly. Whatever was going to happen was somehow her fault. She wasn't even sure why, but she wished ardently that she could stop it now, before it went further.

"I'm glad I seen you goin' by, Jessen," Luke remarked carelessly. "I got a little chore for you. I see you got extry energy for walkin' the long way round with the water tonight, so you can bring up a couple more buckets and wash down these-here cows for me. They had a hard day today. And be sure to get the flies outa their ears and see their feet's nice and clean. And I want you to do—"

"Do it yourself." Jess shrugged. "I'll do camp work, but I'm no servant of yours." With a meaningful look at Torrie where she sat on the milking stool, he turned away.

"You want me to make that an order?" Luke raised his voice.

Slowly Jess turned back to confront them. In a tone as quiet as the hot side of an ember, he said, "You don't give me orders. But if you want to try convincing me, I'll be pleased to fight you—wrastling, bare knuckles, or free style. And if you'd rather not get your looks scrambled, for fear the girls won't make over you so much, I'll race you for stakes—my horse against yours, with the order-taking thrown in just to give you fair odds."

Luke had come up slowly off the wagon tongue where he'd been perched. The two of them were about the same height, but the redhead had the better of Jess by thirty pounds, at least.

"You wouldn't want me to look like a bully, would you?" Luke sneered. "Me wrastlin' you wouldn't hardly seem fair. Besides, I'd hate to see us with a crippled-up driver, not when we're tryin' to make time. So I'll tell you what. I'll delay the pleasure of tearin' you apart limb from limb, like a fried chicken, until you build up some muscle, but in the meantime I could use another horse and these-here folks could use a good laugh, so lead out that piece of crowbait of yours. You're on!"

Three or four of the men had come up by this time, drawn by the loud carry of Luke's voice and scenting a fight. Now they whooped and set off around the circle of wagons to summon the rest—there was not a man among them that didn't enjoy a horse race.

Torrie was stunned by the swiftness with which it had happened. Anxiously she watched Jess go across to get the mare. Father had been graining it along with old Blackie

76

and there was a little more meat on its bones, but it still was hardly any match for Luke's big buckskin. For all that Torrie smarted under Jess's disdain, she realized that she didn't want him to lose that horse. It was actually the only friend he had in his curious lonely world.

As word of the race went around, the rest of the train gathered quickly. They were setting up torches along a straightaway stretch and somebody was stepping off a quarter-mile. Torrie wanted to slip out of the focus of attention, but Luke wouldn't let her.

"Don't run away," he said, "this race is bein' run for you, madam." He chucked her under the chin with a freshness that startled her, as if somehow he considered her his property. "Least you can do," he went on, "is give me one of them smiles of yours for luck. Fact is, you're gonna stand there at the finish line and hold the tape so's I can see you there cheerin' for me all the way."

They had tied the girls' hair ribbons together in one long strand to stretch across the finish line and, unwillingly, Torrie found herself being led forward by Luke, one end of the ribbon thrust in her hand, while one of the other girls was stationed opposite.

"Hold it good and wish me luck," he whispered, "and the first order I'm gonna give that boy is to get down on his knees and apologize for all his rudeness to the fairest young lady in this camp."

"Oh no!" Torrie gasped.

"Yes sir. Right in front of ever'body he's gonna do it. And then I'm gonna collect a little prize from you in private, like maybe a kiss, eh?" Before she could answer, Luke had put the spurs to his horse and the big buckskin leaped away.

As the two men rode down between the rows of on-lookers, they were bombarded by catcalls and advice, rude comments about the mare's condition, and shouts of "Good luck, Luke!" and "Bust on down there now!" Since Jess never had mingled at all with any of the crowd, they were quick to take sides against him.

The two made an odd contrast as they went—Luke stiffly upright in his heavy Spanish saddle, elbows out, chin tucked in, while the buckskin cavorted and sidled in the grandest manner possible. Jess, on the other hand, sat the mare's bare back loosely, legs dangling, for all the world like any farm boy herding the cows home at sundown.

At the starting post, one of the men had a gun. Torrie saw him raise it. The horses were in position—

At the shot, the mare broke fast and flattened out into a dead run that left Luke's horse a half-length behind. Luke rode bunched over, digging the spurs in, the whip flailing. Jess, without a saddle, was molded along the mare's wiry body as if he were part of it. Suddenly under the pain of the spurs, the buckskin threw its head wildly and broke stride, losing ground. Luke yanked its head down furiously and laid on the whip—the horse surged forward, but it obviously would never catch the mare, who seemed to skitter over the ground as if she weren't quite earth-bound. Jess pounded home a good two lengths ahead, ripping the strip of ribbon from Torrie's hand as he thundered past.

Confused, half-deafened by the shouting, Torrie felt hot tears of relief well up and spill down her cheeks. In a daze, she saw Luke haul the buckskin to a trembling halt.

"It was a foul!" he snarled. "Jessen broke early."

"No, he didn't." The starter had ridden up now and shook his head, staring at the mare wonderingly. "He broke

78

a second after you did. It's just that his critter got lightning in her feet."

Jess had walked the mare back and now he slid off. Paying little heed to the men, either those now slapping his back, or the others grumbling to have lost their bets, he stared straight at Luke.

"You can take the saddle and bridle off," he said. "They weren't part of the deal."

Egan's face went livid as he yanked the saddle and began to unbuckle the bridle. Torrie saw that the bit was bright red, the buckskin's mouth badly cut. All at once, she felt sick inside and had to get away. She had to think about what had happened—and why it had happened. Turning blindly, she made her way out of the press of people and rushed—almost ran—off into the summer darkness.

She didn't stop until she reached the brow of the low ridge behind the campground. Hesitating there, trembling, she looked out across the country beyond, lying silent with the moonlight making odd shapes that seemed to lurk behind every bush. She thought of Indians—and yet, she couldn't go back down to the wagons—not yet.

She sank onto a rock, hugging her knees, listening for any sound. It was far enough from camp that none of the noise reached her—the people moving back and forth down there in the last glow of the firelight seemed small and unreal. All of it was unreal—this valley, broad and shadowy in the darkness, stretching away to the east and west as far as she could see, flanked by its distant moon-silvered bluffs. Or was it the realest thing in the world, this terrible fierce land? Sun-drenched by day, the dry hills sending off shivering reflections that distorted everything, alkali dust sifting upward from the oxen's feet, the screech of the tormented parched axles. And by night almost cruelly brilliant with moonlight—the air either split by the weird baying of coyotes or, like this, silent with a stillness that rang in your ears. On the drift of the wind, Torrie caught the scent of a new smell—and yet it was familiar too, something like cookery. . . . Sage. But ten times stronger than the delicate odor of Mother's spice box.

Everything was stronger, harsher, more violent, here in this wilderness. The sudden storms, the throbbing heat, even the people—her own family. They were like foreigners to her. Or was it herself who had turned strange and unfamiliar? Had she ever known herself, she wondered acutely. It was almost as if she were waking out of some long romantic dream, jolted out of it by that moment of hurtling hoofs and the sight of a horse's mouth, dripping blood.

Confused, frightened, she saw Luke Egan again, laying on that whip. She shuddered when she thought of what he might have done to torment Jess if he'd won. She didn't dare imagine it, but the Virginian had. He'd known what the stakes were and how the race would be run. And he'd known from the beginning that Luke Egan was a harsh man, dangerous to play with. That's what he had meant when he'd told Father there would be a fight—he'd looked at Torrie because somehow he had known she would spark it. Sick with humiliation, she realized that everyone had known, everyone except herself. How she could have been so fatuous as to welcome Luke's arrogance and try to defend his bullying humor! Milked his cows for the chance to speak with him. A whole new hot embarrassment flooded over her at the very thought. Just because some hoydenish young women of the camp considered Luke desirable, she had lowered herself to compete with them —she'd actually been coquetting Luke! And, what was worst of all, she had succeeded. He was spending more time with her every day, and even getting jealous. This business of picking a fight with Jess proved it. But how do you stop the whole thing once it's started? she wondered miserably.

It made her remember how she and the girls at home had talked so often about men, how they would make conquests some day. They had practiced their smiles and downcast glances in front of a mirror and teased each other about who would be married first. But they never had imagined in their daydreams that it could turn into a big hostile problem. They hadn't plotted any strategy for retreat. Miserably Torrie racked her brain for some way to ease out of Luke's affections—some kind way—

A small sound roused her and she realized that someone was walking up the hill from the direction of camp. Instantly alert, Torrie glanced around, her breath sticking in her throat. Of course, it was probably just someone of the train, but if there had been any place to hide—! There wasn't; the hilltop was almost as bright as day under the full moon.

"Thought I seen you slip off this way," Luke spoke out from a short distance away. "I reckoned you must have come up here to wait for me, and give me that little prize I didn't win."

Torrie saw him now, looming up like a hulking shadow. She scrambled to her feet and stood uncertainly as he came on. Too soon—it was going to come to a showdown too soon, before she was ready! Swiftly Torrie knew it, from some tone in his voice, and his words struck a new uneasiness in her.

When he reached her side, he stood looking down at her. "You!" he said softly, and she realized he was furious. "Should have knowed you weren't as innercent as you look, with that baby smile. Act like a wide-eyed little school kid, tryin' to play grown up. Well, I'll say you had me fooled, if that's any satisfaction. Only when I get through, you won't be so pleased—"

She tried to edge away, but he caught her wrist roughly and jerked her around to face him.

"I—d-d-don't know what you mean—" Torrie stammered.

"Oh, you d-d-don't?" he mimicked. "You can leave off the act. Luke Egan only gets took once. You helped 'em trick me outa my horse, but—"

"I did?" Torrie stared at him bewildered.

"Don't put on that helpless look. 'Course you did. You knew Jessen's mare was a racer. Your pap knew it too—I seen him collectin' money after the race. That towhead walked off with the best horse I ever straddled, and you set it up. Guess you thought you'd have a good laugh, all of you."

" I didn't set up anything." Torrie tried to speak firmly, but her voice was shaky.

"Shut your lyin' mouth!" With a swift movement of his hand, Luke slapped her full across the face. Then savagely he jerked her to him and planted his lips on hers, pinning her arms helpless in spite of her struggles. "That's my little prize," he muttered. "And now—"

"And now, nothing." Someone else had spoken, Torrie realized dimly, shaken by the blow and still paralyzed by Luke's grip. With an oath, he thrust her from him and turned to meet the newcomer.

"Bait!" he yelled wildly. "So she baited another trap!"

"She didn't trap you," Jessen said. "I saw you leave and followed."

From the ground where she had fallen to her hands and knees, Torrie saw him now, standing there, his blond top silvery white under the cold blaze of the moon. With that nightmare feeling of being glued down, she watched as Luke started to circle, half-crouching, his big ruthless hands spread to attack.

Jess stood still and ready. "Come on, Luke," he coaxed gently. "I just saw you manhandle a kid, so I know you got no real conscience about tackling me. There's nobody around now to call you bully—or hero either."

With a rush, Egan swarmed onto him. They grappled and there was a flurry of elbows and boots.

"Free style—?" Jess spoke as cool as water. "All right." And with a sudden twist, he flipped the redhead over his shoulder to land on his back with a thud that shook the ground.

Jess didn't press his advantage but stood back and waited. As Egan struggled up, Torrie saw his hand slide into his shirt front, halfway drawing an ugly pistol. At the same instant, Jess quickly reached inside the back of his collar, and when his hand came out, cocked, there was a gleam of thin steel in it.

"Any way you want it," he remarked. "Go on and draw that gun, we'll see if I can throw this knife faster'n you can trigger."

83

The moment seemed to last forever; then Luke's hand came slowly out into the open and it was empty. Straightening up, he glanced down the slope toward the camp, where splinters of light were beginning to spread out from the wagons—lanterns weaving through the darkness.

"Looks like your friends are comin' to save you," he sneered.

"I got no friends," Jess said curtly, "and I don't need saving." Sheathing the knife, he stood, hands hanging. "I'm waiting for you."

Abruptly Egan cursed. "You ain't worth bustin' a knuckle on. Take your flirty little filly home and tell her pap she ain't welcome with this train, and neither are you. Come to think of it, he ain't either. That's the verdict of the captain and the vice-captain and justice of the court, all of which is me. Tell him, far as I care, you can all go get swallowed up in the quicksand." He stomped off down the hill.

Slowly Jess walked to where Torrie still huddled on the ground. Not too kindly, he asked, "Are you hurt?"

"No," she quavered.

He held out a hand, pulled her to her feet unceremoniously. "Then come on."

"Jess—" She had to hurry to keep up with him as he started down off the ridge. "Jess, I'm—I'm grateful you came when you did."

"Are you?" He kept on walking.

"He was— I don't know what he was going to do!"

"No," he snorted in disgust. "I guess you don't. You don't know much about men at all."

She took this in meek silence. In a minute, she asked timidly, "Those lights—are they looking for us?"

84

"Looking for you."

"Were you searching for me too?"

"It's part of my job. Don't get any ideas," he told her. Then he added, "Only difference was, I knew how to find you. I just followed Luke."

"I didn't ask him—" She hesitated. "I mean I didn't go off to meet him. He surprised me up there. Honestly!"

Jess didn't answer.

She looked again at the lights, coming nearer all the time. "What are you going to tell them?"

"Me?" He made a small angry sound. "I'm going to tell 'em nothing. You're the one with the explaining to do."

"Jess, help me—" she pleaded swiftly. The lights were getting close ahead of them. "I don't want to answer questions in front of everybody!"

He checked suddenly to turn upon her. When he spoke, his voice was strained with suppressed exasperation. "That's the worst of it. The rock-bottom worst. When Luke said you were a little kid trying to play fancy lady, he was right. Oh sure, I heard that—I heard the whole thing. Your pa's got an idea that folks ought to learn by experience. I was just waiting to see if it would work. Leastways I waited as long as I could. I should have known you couldn't handle a buck like Egan. All this time joshing you, and you never tumbled to it. You really thought he was courting you—him, the cock of the camp?"

The words lashed against her with the shock of cold rain. Inwardly, Torrie wrinkled like wet tissue paper as she listened to him.

"I'm going to tell you something," he went on in a quick low voice, for the searchers were calling back and forth not too far away now. "Your pa's notions may be all right about experience and all that, but I got the feeling when anybody's as young-blind as you are, they need to be told. So I'll tell you: Luke was making sport of you for the rest of 'em to laugh. Pretending to pay you attention so you'd calf-eye him some more. He was getting back at your pa, because your pa's a bigger man than he'll ever be. And you just walked into it headfirst." He took hold of her arm almost as roughly as Luke had. "Your pa's been decent to me—it's the only reason I'm saying this. If you don't want to hurt him, then put on a sunbonnet and stay under it until you grow up some." Fiercely he released her and walked forward toward the lights.

Somebody spotted them. "There's Jessen!"

"He's got the girl!" the shout went up.

"Is she all right?"

"She's feeling some poorly," said Jess, without hesitation. "Dizzy spell come on her while she was out taking a walk, she had to sit down for a while, that's all." And before Torrie knew it, he had steered her between the converging lanterns and they were hurrying on to the wagon.

There was a red mark on Torrie's face where Luke had struck her; Father kept looking at it as they sat together in the wagon with the lantern turned low, and Jess told them in hushed tones exactly what had happened. For all that he had warned Torrie she'd have to do her own explaining, she had halted and stumbled so that finally Jess took up the story. It was plain he didn't intend to gloss over anything with Thomas, but he did say that when he followed Egan, from the way he had wandered around, it was pretty plain there was no meeting set up. He was out searching.

86

When he'd finished, they sat silent. Mother had shifted to sit a little closer to Torrie, and now, quite unexpectedly, she put out a hand and took the girl's, with a firm reassurance that brought tears of gratitude to Torrie's eyes.

Father sat silent and stern.

It was Cal who finally broke the stillness. "Where's your knife now? I don't see it?"

"It's where it'll come in handy," Jess told him shortly.

"I'm glad you didn't have to throw it," Liza murmured.

"Yes'm, so am I," said Jess. "I never thrown a knife in my life."

It made Torrie look up at him swiftly, aware all over again of the near damage she had wrought. Jess looked back, and as he met her eyes, this time there was no mockery.

They sat a while in stillness that swelled with unspoken thoughts.

"You reckon Luke'll get over his meanness by morning?" Liza asked finally.

"That," said Father in a curious tight voice, "is not the point. Tomorrow when they are ready to leave, I will forestall any further question by stating that we have illness and intend to wait for the next train. It's a subterfuge and a lie, but it's to be preferred, in this case, to frank discussion. I believe that, at one uncouth word from Luke Egan, I may kill him."

II

Torrie stayed in bed that next morning as the rest of the train broke camp. Huddled down under the sheets in spite of the mounting warmth, she put her fingers in her ears and closed her eyes. But nothing could shut out her imaginings; she could just guess what sort of big tales Luke was telling about her—she could almost hear the titters of the other girls.

Somehow the thing that hurt the most was that he had kissed her. For years, Torrie had dreamed about that first kiss and what it would be like and who the man would be. She'd always assumed it would be the man she was going to marry some day—a beautiful close personal moment. Instead, she felt like scrubbing her mouth whenever she remembered it—the harsh hold he'd clamped on her, and the scornful way he'd forced the embrace on her in angry vengeance. It made her feel soiled. . . .

"They've gone now," Liza called in to her. "If you lie there under those covers, you're like to come on with a fever." The same old scolding manner. And yet, for a moment last night, Torrie had felt near to her mother. Disconsolately she got up and dressed. It was getting hot in the wagon, and by the time she had climbed out the sun was high.

Their little camp seemed dreadfully alone. All that was left of the train was a dust haze that hung on the still air, up along the river's edge, growing more distant every minute.

It was so breathless that even the leaves drooped, motionless, on the willows down in the bottoms. There were no cottonwoods along here, either—nowhere to go for shade. The oxen were tied down in the brush, but it was too thick to drive the wagon in, too full of insects.

Liza was bending over a scrub pail, washing her towels and dishrags, that kind of nervous work that she always plunged into when she was worried.

Haltingly, Torrie asked, "Where are Father and—the others?"

88

"They've ridden up to the bluffs to see if they can sight another train." Mother spoke even a little shorter than usual.

"I guess everybody's just disgusted with me," Torrie mumbled.

Liza glanced up at her a minute, and the anxious frown softened a little. "Maybe it's me they should blame," she said. "I saw this coming way back home. You been in such a hurry to take up with men, seemed like you lost your senses. Your pa kept saying you'd grow out of it, just like he thinks Caleb will straighten up, but sometimes I think it'd be easier on a body to get shook out of it." There was no anger in the way she said it, and, for once, Torrie felt comforted just by Mother's native bluntness. She couldn't have stood to be lied to or even soothed just then.

"I keep thinking," she said, "how Father might have really killed Luke if he'd been up on the hill." It seemed an incredible thought, but she'd never heard her father exaggerate.

Liza nodded. "Likely he would. And Jess could certain-sure have been hurt bad if Luke wasn't such a coward. There's been a lot of men got hurt over women, and it never does anybody any good in the end. But don't keep fretting over it. It's done and you learned something every girl's got to find out sooner or later, which is that men go rough inside quicker'n women do. They got to be handled careful. Learning how takes time." And she went back to her work.

Torrie looked across at the barren bluffs shimmering with heat waves and saw the men coming back, Cal riding behind Father on Blackie, Jess on the buckskin, handling him with just a halter. Torrie wondered as she watched them come—the Virginian's way with animals was almost uncanny. He seemed to speak some language they could understand. How many times she'd seen the buckskin rear and act up with Luke, so that it seemed to take all the ability in the world for him to sit the saddle. And yet here the horse came stepping along gently with Jess—no show at all. Ruefully, Torrie realized that a few days before this would have filled her with contempt.

As they dismounted, Father shook his head in answer to Liza's questioning look.

"Nothing in sight along the back trail. I'm afraid most of the trains are ahead of us. Of course, we know from what the St. Louis courier told us the other day that Colonel Carroll is back there some six days' travel behind us, but—"

"Tell 'em about the smoke," Cal said meanly.

Father looked at the boy with a frown, and Jess made a small inarticulate sound that might have been irritation. Obviously Cal had brought up a subject they hadn't intended to mention.

"What smoke?" Liza asked tensely.

"I'm sorry to have to say that from the top of the bluff we did see some smoke." Father took off his hat and mopped at his balding head. "Far off to the north. . . ."

"It was coming in puffs." Cal grinned fearfully. "It was Injun signals."

Jess turned away and led the horses down to the river to water them. The others stood silent—they were all thinking of the rider who had come past a few days earlier from Fort Laramie, headed back toward the States. He had reported that the Sioux were gathering, getting ready to go on the warpath.

"I doubt if we're very deep in the Sioux country." Father

90

tried to sound reassuring. "However, I don't like the thought of venturing on alone. The river, too, will be impossible to cross without help if its bottom continues to be largely quicksand. And yet we can ill afford to stay here long. Every day lost at this end of the trail will make us a day later at the other end."

"And if we all get scalped, we won't ever get there," added Cal warmly, giving Torrie a nasty glance.

"Somebody's talking almighty big," observed Mother.

"There's no denying that we are in a rather unpleasant predicament," Thomas said. He didn't look at Torrie, but the unspoken blame was harder to take than if he'd ranted at her.

The sun had become almost nerve-racking. By common consent they took refuge in the wagon, which wasn't much relief, although it did protect them from the fierce noonday rays. Jess had come back from tending the stock now and paused to look in at them.

"Anything you want me to do?" he asked.

"Do? What's to do?" Liza snapped peevishly.

Without a word, Jess ducked under the wagon out of sight.

Father looked troubled. "Our situation," he said slowly, "will not be improved by temper or panic. Emotion in such circumstances as ours can only be destructive, and the worst thing that can happen is to allow fear to drive us apart. We must try to focus on some positive course of action. . . ."

"But it's so HOT!" yelled Cal wildly, glaring at Torrie. "Let's go on. At least there's some breeze when you're moving."

"This is exactly what I meant by the danger of becoming overexcited." Father tried to speak evenly, but it was evidently taking some effort. "We must try to put our physical discomfort aside—"

"I don't care!" Cal ranted. "I'm hot. I'm getting out of here. I'll bet it's cooler down under with Jess." Scrambling over them pell-mell, he crawled out the rear opening and disappeared beneath the wagon.

Thomas looked at Liza. "Patience, my dear. I believe the boy was badly frightened by the sight of those smoke signals. This fury is sheer reaction—"

He was interrupted by a hoot from below, a screech of laughter. A second later, Cal appeared at the tailgate, still roaring with derision.

"Jess—! He's—! You know what he's doing? He's writing little baby words in the dust. C—A—T." Cal burbled with the ridiculousness of it. "He can't even spell 'horse.' "

"Caleb!" Father's voice thundered through the stream of high-pitched mockery.

Cal broke off, still grimacing with his unkindly humor. "Well, it's funny," he said, a little less boisterously.

And then Jess swung out from under the wagon and stood up. In the brilliance of the sunlight, his pale blue eyes were wide open, he wasn't trying to hide the steady judgment in them. For a long minute, he looked around at the family grouped rigidly in the rear of the wagon.

Then, without emphasis, without the least touch of insolence, he said to Thomas, "I reckon you were right, sir. There's a plenty that can't be learned from books."

Leaving that curious sentence with them, he walked away, down to the trees. Unhurriedly he led out the mare, hitched himself across her back, and swung astraddle. As he headed her out along the back trail, eastward, he put her into a long trot that left a wreath of dust hanging in the air behind him.

Father was the first to move. Stiffly, as if he were older than Grandpa, he got down out of the wagon. Briefly he looked at Caleb as if he disliked what he saw, then turned to speak to all of them.

"Jess was referring to a remark I made a long time ago when he came to me in Independence. When he asked to hire on, he told me honestly and humbly that he could neither read nor write. I, of course, pointed out to him that many great qualities can exist in a man whose formal education has been neglected. Now he has quite appropriately returned the thought to me in reverse. Education does not, of itself, stimulate decency and gentility. Or didn't you understand what he meant?" He studied them bleakly.

Liza was looking after the diminishing horseback figure with an expression of painful recognition. "So that was it!" she muttered softly. "All this time I been blaming the boy for holding himself too proud to mix with us. I should have guessed—" She turned to her husband. "It would have helped if you'd told us. It would have explained why he never took so much as a cup of coffee at our table. Who'd have known it was from modesty?"

"It didn't occur to me that there could be any question about it." Thomas still surveyed them, unsmiling. Without his gold-rimmed glasses, his face haggard, hands knotted hard at his sides, there was a fierceness about him that had nothing to do with the slenderness of his slight body.

"Why?" he demanded. "Why should a man's secret need be told, if he's among intelligent people of good will? I had thought our family big enough to rise above petty curiosity, much less to indulge in censure of what they do not under-

93

stand. Jess asked me to keep his story in confidence, but, now that part of it is discovered, it would be less than fair to leave the remainder untold. There were no schools where he grew up. His parents were illiterate. It makes learning seem somewhat more precious to a man. It makes him want to work for it. I suppose Jess will always appreciate what education he receives a hundred times more than someone"—he glanced at Cal—"who had it handed to him freely to use or misuse, or not to use at all. When Jess offered to barter his labor on this trip in return for what teaching I could give him, I admired him for it. What little I've been able to show him so far while we were herding together, he has absorbed with eagerness and gratitude. He's made good progress, thanks to his ardent application. It has proven a bitter contrast to the attitudes of my own feckless offspring."

Grimly he looked at Torrie. "I'm sorry, my child, to have to include you in my disillusionment, inasmuch as your error springs from immaturity. But it also results from a lack of imagination, which I had not expected in you. I trust by now you realize that, because you made a public spectacle of yourself, I have been deprived of my natural right to call Egan to account for his treatment of you. This is a bitter pill for a parent to swallow. Cal"— he turned again to the boy—"has been even more of a disappointment. Lazy, rude, and fretful—all childish manifestations. I was hoping he'd pull up out of them. It would have shown character if he had learned to curb himself. He hasn't. And this today—a malicious show of derision heaped upon another member of our party—this is no childish foible. It shows genuine and shameful insensitivity." Thomas took a deep tremulous breath.

94

"One of the reasons," he went on almost sorrowfully, "that I felt we must make this trip was to learn, under pressure perhaps, what our natural capacities are. I believed our lives were too sheltered in St. Louis to develop whatever greatness may lie dormant in us. Instead, I find that what the travel has developed is a shocking smallness that leads me to censure myself for the way I've brought up my children. I see now that pure reasoning is not always strong enough incentive to produce dignity and tolerance. Let us trust that it is not too late to start afresh. Caleb, you will walk with me to the willows yonder."

Cal had looked increasingly uncomfortable at the contained fury of his father's quiet words; now he went white and disbelieving. With sudden ire, Thomas seized upon his collar, spun him around, and marched him down into the underbrush, leaving Torrie and her mother silent under the echo of his indictment.

As dusk settled in to quench the molten brass of the sunset sky, the heat lessened to where it was bearable to move about, and Liza went silently to work, fixing a stew of dried buffalo meat, while Torrie milked the cow and Caleb and Father tended the stock. There was no conversation—no flat comments from Liza or tartness from Cal, no scholarly remarks from Thomas Anders. In the strained unnatural silence, each individual seemed bound up in private thoughts through which ran four separate but parallel threads of remorse that kept them all glancing back along the empty trail.

It had been that way all day. Father had sat in the meager shade of the wagon, paging through his book of poetry.

He didn't appear to be reading, just turning the leaves as a man will touch a familiar possession, for reassurance. The terrible look had not gone from his face—an expression of hurt, the recognition of failure. It made Torrie want to cry. She would have liked to let go and weep—it would have relieved some of the tight ache inside her—but, for the first time in her life, her unhappiness was too great to come out in tears.

Looking at Caleb who had sat under the wagon all day, doing his lessons with a puckered face, she almost wished Father had taken his displeasure out on her the same way. A willow switch would have been easier to bear than this sick sense of loss that overwhelmed her every time she looked at her father. It was as if they'd lost the train and Jess and Father, too.

For the thousandth time, Torrie searched the darkening valley to the eastward. Just at sundown, she had thought she'd noticed a rise of dust far off downriver, but now she was afraid it might have been her imagination.

"Do you want supper, Thomas?" Mother asked, as he came up to the fire.

Father shook his head slightly. "Not yet." For a minute they all stood quiet, listening. And then Torrie straightened sharply. Almost at the same instant the others heard it too —the soft sound of a horse's hoofs coming along the powdery bed of the trail. Mother ran to light the lantern; she held it up as Jess rode in.

He slid off the mare's back wearily, his face so caked with sweat and dust, it was impossible to read his expression. Thomas went to meet him.

"Jess—" he began, in an unnatural voice.

"Yes, sir," Jess spoke ahead of him, as if determined to

96

ignore the stress in all their faces. "I reckon you about gave me up, but you see, I thought I ought to keep going until I sighted another train—you need to know whether to wait or not."

"Quite right." Father laid a hand on his shoulder as if to make sure he was real. "You were absolutely right!" he repeated emphatically.

"Well, there's one coming along," Jess said, "but it's a good piece back there. Probably be two days getting here if it doesn't bog down somewhere in between."

"That's better than I'd hoped," Father said seriously. "We'll wait for them rather than venture on deeper into Sioux territory alone."

"Whatever you decide." Jess nodded. He turned to lead the mare down to the river.

Caleb had hung in the background, but now he rushed to place himself in front of Jess. For a second he couldn't get a word out. Then convulsively he said, "Could I water your horse?"

Slowly Jess handed him the end of the halter rope. "Don't let her drink too much while she's hot."

"I'll walk her!" Cal offered, almost tearfully eager. "I'll just walk her a little until she cools off!"

It broke the tension. In the lantern light, Torrie thought she saw a quirk at the corners of Jess's mouth, the nearest she'd ever seen him come to a smile.

Mother was hustling around the fire. "We waited supper," she said. Then, straightening up, she looked at the Virginian. "That is—we'd be pleased if you'll sit down with us."

Jess hesitated, then nodded. "Thank you, ma'am."

Coming over to the wagon, he took up the wash bucket

from beneath and set it on the bottom step, rolled up his shirt sleeves, glancing at Torrie who had stood back in sudden shyness. She watched him sluice the dirt off his face and arms, and, when he groped for the towel, she put it in his hand. As he dried off, he stood studying her thoughtfully.

"Maybe you wish I'd just kited out and not come back," he said in that irreverent way of his, as if he were somehow challenging her. "Did you think I'd quit in the middle of the job?"

"I wouldn't have blamed you," she told him in a low voice. "Why should you bother to help a crazy family like this?"

The words brought a startling change over him. The defiant look eased, and this time he did smile. Reaching out, he took the end of one of her long braids and pulled it lightly.

"I'd hate to see that hanging on some Injun's belt," he said.

CROSSROADS

FORT LARAMIE. Six hundred and forty miles out of Independence, thirteen hundred yet to go—or fourteen hundred—or fifteen hundred. Nobody had ever calculated it perfectly.

June almost over and July not yet begun. Most of the travelers who had paused here at the crossroads of the wilderness, to rest and breathe and reprovision, were glad enough of the new feel of mountain coolness in the air. But the old-timers, the traders up from Santa Fe, the mountain men who traveled westward as guides to some of the trains—they were watching the sky.

Innocent little cottony clouds kept gathering on the western horizon, drifting eastward on some higher current of wind that never reached the ground, dropping a fierce little shower sometimes on the tired multitude that grouped around the whitewashed adobe walls of the Fort. If there was a sudden shivery draft in the evenings, the emigrants just thanked heaven for it. But the mountain men looked at heaven with a critical eye, and watched for the rising of the Dog Star.

For the others, Laramie itself was the big excitement, drowning out thoughts about the weather. The emigrants were more fascinated with the Sioux. Encamped all over the banks of little Laramie Creek, where it ran into the Platte, they had come in families and whole villages, had set up their lodges, unpacked their children, and turned loose their stock. It was a screaming barking whooping melee. Painted bucks were everywhere, more vividly colored than the wild little pinto ponies they rode. War dances were held every night, but not against the white man. It was the Shoshoni they were after, and they made an unearthly lot of noise about it. The men shouted and yipped, ponies whinnied, craggy old women screeched at the children and the dogs—well, there were dogs all over the place. Fighting, yapping, snapping, some of them working— pulling pack loads on a travois, or drag-cart made of sticks. Rumors said that the dogs even graced the stewpots of the Indians when food was scarce.

It wasn't too hard to believe, in view of the prices at the Fort. Flour a dollar a pound! More than one wife closed her purse and turned away, vowing to make bread out of wild grass seed before she'd pay such an amount. Other items couldn't be shrugged off, though. Tea. Sugar. Cornmeal. Lard— Torrie remembered how Grandpa had told them over and over to be sure and stock plenty of lard, or their diet of dried meat would never hold them up.

She'd been thinking of Grandpa a good deal these last days; she missed him acutely sometimes. And now the whole memory of him was brought back by this coincidence—you couldn't call it anything but a completely fantastic coincidence. Out here in the middle of nowhere, they had run into someone who actually knew Grandpa!

100

Father had met the man, an old trapper, at the Fort and had brought him to the wagon to meet Mother.

"So you're Silas Pickett's daughter." He took Liza's hand with the beautiful grace of the woodsman, a warm unstudied gesture. "Certainly I remember your pa, came over there to Illinois to help us fight old Black Hawk back in the thirties. I'm glad to know he's still alive and makin' that applejack of his." There was an ageless vigor about this Jim Clyman that reminded Torrie of Grandpa's own sinewy energy. Hard-muscled and sunburned, he had the look of a man who had moved along the mountain trails for so long he had forgotten how to be tired.

He was on his way east, just stopped at the Fort to trade "howdies" and get back into the feel of speaking good United States American, he said. It turned out he had just come from California.

This whetted their interest so that they couldn't let him go without a little talk. And so for a while he sat with them around the campfire with the afternoon shadows stretching down from the bluffs behind the Fort and the ecstatic racket of the drunken Indians all around them, while Mother made coffee from her small precious stock of it, and Father asked questions.

"I hear that Hastings himself is waiting at Fort Bridger to take the California parties through," he said. "Could that be true?"

"That's right." Clyman nodded. "Him and me traveled together that far from California."

"I trust that he's a better guide than his book." Father frowned. "It has proven to be not entirely accurate in some respects. For instance, it assured us of plentiful grazing and firewood all along the Platte, whereas in this last stretch we just crossed there was hardly a blade of grass left. And as for firewood, we've been burning buffalo chips ever since we left the Kansas."

"Don't doubt it." Clyman smiled dryly. "Hastings gets fairly lathered up when he starts to write about how easy it is to get to California. You dead-set on California?" He shot a glance around the circle at the four Anderses and Jess, who sat back just enough to seem withdrawn from the family group.

"Yes," Father answered, "we hope to settle somewhere near Mr. Sutter's Fort. I had supposed that area would be fairly well populated with our own kind."

"Will be, I reckon, when this emigration gets there." The mountain man saucered some of his coffee and blew on it delicately to cool it. "Sutter's all right. You can count on him to treat you tolerable fair. At least he wouldn't rather see you starve than owe him money, which is more'n I could say for most traders."

"As I understand it, Mr. Hastings is in his employ?"

"Hastings works for Hastings," Clyman told them flatly. "He'll likely try to sell you land—that's what he's aimin' at, which is what makes him lean so heavy on the finer aspects of California, as you might imagine."

"I see." Father rubbed his chin thoughtfully.

"How soon will he be leaving Bridger with his train?" Liza wanted to know.

"Soon, ma'am." Clyman sounded just a trace sardonic. "At least it better be soon or he won't make it over the Sierra afore snow. 'Course when I left there, hadn't any emigrants come through yet, but they're startin' to roll in there about now. I'd say he'll take his train west afore the end of July. You could make it, if you travel fast. But if you get to Bridger later'n August first, you better take the Soda Springs route and make no mistake about it."

"I don't understand. Hastings' new trail is shorter than the old way past Soda Springs, isn't it?" Father asked, puzzled. "We'd been counting on saving a good four hundred miles by taking his cutoff."

"Probably somewhat of an exaggeration." Clyman drained off the rest of his coffee. "Just between you'n me, Hastings had never been over this short cut of his when he wrote his book. Him and me just came across it west-to-east this spring, and I tell you, sir, it's a tough one. Hastings thinks he'll make it back with the wagon train, but I'm not so sure. If he does, it's not going to save much time, if any, and you may be more dead than alive when you get there. I'll tell you: there's the Wasatch Mountains to get across first, and we found no way that wagons could be brought through except hoisted by hand, winched and tackled, and dragged along stream beds. It was even a hard pitch on horseback. West of that comes the worst stretch of desert I ever crossed, just west of the Great Salt Lake—nothin' but salt flat, no water for fifty, sixty miles or more. . . ."

"But he assured us of water at the end of the first day's travel!" Father spoke with increasing dismay.

"Like I said, that was writ before he ever saw the country. Now after you leave the salt flats," Clyman picked up a stick and smoothed out a place in the dust, "there's still a rough stretch over to the Humboldt. If I was you, sir, I'd stick to the proven route." He leaned forward and drew a crude map in the dust while the others moved in closer to watch.

"When you leave Laramie you follow on up the Platte until you reach a bad canyon that can't be got through, have to go overland across a rough stretch of alkali desert. Carry all the water you can. Then you pick up the Sweetwater River, and it's easy going over South Pass and down to Fort Bridger, water all the way. Then, at Bridger, you got to choose. The road to Soda Springs, around the north end of the Wasatch, is longer, but it's fair going, plenty of water. There's a stretch of dry land from Fort Hall, after you leave the Snake River, until you pick up the Humboldt, and it's no tea-party, but nothin' to grind you

down like that Salt Desert. Here. Here's your cutoff." He
drew a ragged line and spotted a pebble for Salt Lake. "Like
I said, it's a killer. Sun blazin' off that white stuff, wind
kickin' it up in your face continual, and it ain't solid entirely, most time you'll be axle-deep in it. And no water
—not a drop for man nor beast 'til you get clear to Pilot
Peak on t'other side. By the time you're halfways across,
you start seein' things, horses get spooky—" He shook his
head and got to his feet. "Well, I've got to be shovin' along.

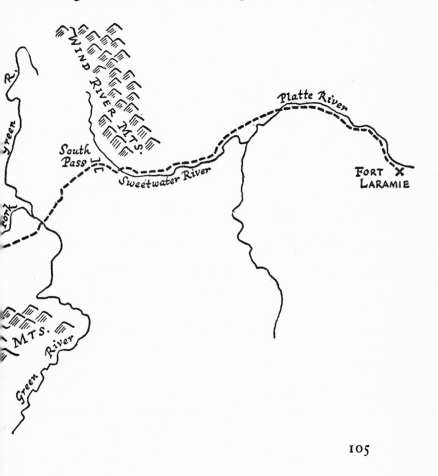

Thanky for the coffee, ma'am, and if I see your pa when I get back east, I'll tell him you've been takin' the trail well."

· The Fort was built in a square around a big central courtyard, and it was there that the travel-worn emigrants, tired and undecided and fearing as they were, thronged together that last evening before most of them took to the trail again. They met under the cool summer night sky—of all things—to dance.

It had been a spontaneous wish, a notion that spread like brushfire through the camp. Men dragged fiddles out of the depths of their wagons; somebody brought along a banjo, and, for all it was just a minstrel accessory, its bright metallic rhythm glittered against the mellower fiddle music and set feet to tapping. Men in patched homespuns swung their wives into line for a reel. Hands struck up the beat, and faces parched by sun and wind and dust lost their squint-eyed haggard look as they honored their partners with a bow and a dip, obeying the caller who shouted to them to "let a little moon shine in your smile!"

Leaving Jess to take care of the wagon, Thomas Anders had brought his family over to watch the fun—he'd said they would only look on for a while, but as the first reel ended and they squared off into sets, some impulse seemed to seize him. Turning to Liza, he said abruptly, "May I have the honor?"

She blinked and half-smiled, then glanced at Torrie and Caleb. "I don't know if we should leave the children. . . ."

"We'll be all right," Torrie told her mechanically. She was actually stunned to think that Mother knew how to dance.

And so the two of them walked out into the yard and took their places in one of the sets, while Torrie and Cal looked on, astounded. This was something that could never have happened at home. But then where was home? she wondered, bewildered. What were the real home characters of people? Were these two being their own selves as they sat by the fire back in St. Louis, lost in their work, blank-eyed and silent? Or was this really them—this lively well-tanned man with a small dark beard (no absent-minded air now) and a woman whose face, if not pretty, was full of warmth and pleasure as she dropped him a curtsy.

> "Swing all hands and circle up four,
> Let that first couple through the door. . . ."

The music started out with a steady skirt-swinging beat, but as the dancers loosened up, it romped along faster. Father's sparse hair was down over his eyes; Mother had a new natural color in her cheeks, and when she locked elbows with a man he knew he'd been swung!

With the dancers sashaying, laughing, whirling, and all around the shrill drive of the music, the caller's strident chant—Torrie felt dizzy. For some reason, tears started to her eyes brought by some strange emotion, almost an ecstasy. She'd never felt this alive before or this close to everybody else in the world.

A cautious nudge in her ribs brought her back to earth, and she turned, mistily, to find Caleb looking up at her.

"Are you sorry you aren't dancing?" he asked soberly. "Do you wish you didn't have to stay with me?"

Fervently she put an arm around his bony shoulders and hugged him. "Of course not! I'm glad to be right here.

Right here!" Only she meant more by it than she could possibly put into words.

"I think dancing is stupid," Cal said bluffly. "Everybody just goes around in circles—"

"But they're having fun. Don't you see? Mother and Father are having *fun*."

He studied the dancers matter-of-factly. "I guess so. But—"

"And they never did before. Did you ever dream they could dance?"

Cal considered this silently.

As the set was ending, a gangling young man walked over and stopped in front of Torrie. Visibly summoning his courage, he said, in a burst, "Ma'am, I know it's for'ard of me to speak, but I'd take it kinely if you'd dance with me."

Speechless, Torrie blushed hotly, overwhelmed with gratitude that someone should offer. Trying hard not to embarrass him, she summoned all her dignity and said gravely, "I'm flattered you asked me, sir, but I'm not allowed yet."

Father and Mother had come up in time to hear. As the fellow saw them, he looked a little apprehensive, but Thomas bowed to him as politely as if they'd both been the same age. "Thank you, sir," he said. "She'll be pleased to be your partner next year."

Mother gave Torrie an approving look and, when the young man had gone, she said, "You did just right."

Father nodded. "But I believe, to forestall a continual bombardment of invitations, we'd better leave."

"No!" Torrie protested so sharply it almost sounded impertinent. Hastily she added, "I want you to stay. You looked so—so—just handsome out there dancing. Cal and I can go back to the wagon alone. It isn't far."

Mother was starting to object, when Father stopped her with a little gesture. "I really would like to have one more dance with you, Liza," he said gently. Turning to Torrie, he went on, "I'm sure you can go home alone, my dear." The old formal courtesy that she had once detested, thinking somehow it had meant lack of affection, now made Torrie feel more grown and full of dignity than ever before. She wondered, in this whirl of new-found perspective, how she could have ever thought harshly of him for his manners.

As Torrie and Cal walked away from the Fort, they could hear the howl of the wolves up on the bluffs and the crazed yip-yip of the Sioux down along the creek, where the flicker of a hundred fires dotted the darkness. How did the Anders family of St. Louis turn up here? she thought helplessly.

But Cal wasn't so plunged in inward confusion. He put out a hand and clutched her arm suddenly in a grip that made her stop dead-still inside.

"Look!"

They had almost reached their own campsite, and Torrie stiffened as she saw what Cal was pointing at. There were a dozen Indians around their wagon; in the light of the lantern, they were milling about the tailgate where they had Jess backed up in a tight spot. One of them was poking a lance playfully at the Virginian's middle ribs, while the others reeled about, jawing at each other in their strange gibberish. The light glinted off their bare shoulders and horribly painted faces.

"I'll get the gun," croaked Cal hoarsely, and started forward, but Torrie caught him and yanked him back.

"No! No! You must run get Father quickly! Hurry!" She shoved him in the direction of the Fort, and after one instant of scowling rebellion, he did as he was told.

One of the Indians had climbed into the wagon; now he reappeared wrapped in a quilt. With a sudden panic, Torrie recognized that it was the quilt with the banknotes sewn inside.

"Put that down!" Jess spoke loud enough for her to hear. He shoved the spear aside boldly and started forward, but two other Indians seized him, pinning his arms. Torrie took a deep breath and walked quickly up into the light.

The Indians seemed surprised to see her, fixing her with their terrible dark eyes, wild as an animal's. She could smell them now, rank with grease and liquor—an odor she would never forget.

When he saw her, Jess shook his head sharply to warn her off, but she walked on into the midst of them. The big buck with the quilt had draped it around himself and was capering around foolishly, staggering as he danced.

Quickly Torrie climbed up into the wagon, went to the front, and rummaged in a place behind the mahogany bureau, a private niche where she had put her own satchel of personal belongings and two other things—her mother's silk party dress and the white satin hat. In all this time no one had discovered them there. Now, climbing back out of the wagon, she walked straight up to the Indian who had the quilt.

"These are better," she said loudly, although she didn't expect him to understand her. "Here. Take these—" She held them out.

He took the silk dress, fingering it with a gleam of delight in his dark face. But when he reached for the white satin hat, she held it behind her.

"No!" she cried. "Give me the quilt first. The quilt—"

"Torrie, let him have whatever he wants!" Jess called to her in a voice half-strangled with anxiety.

"Give me the quilt! Give it!" she insisted desperately. And as the Indian wavered in front of her, she reached out and snatched it from him, at the same moment shoving the wedding hat into his hands.

Foggily he took it, ran a long dirty finger over its smoothness, then seized it and jammed it down on his head. Draping the dress around his shoulders, he strutted before the others in a way that could have been funny, seen at a safer distance. Torrie took the chance to fling the comforter in back of her, far into the shadows under the wagon.

The other Indians were coming forward now, starting to press around her, their hands stretched out, obviously demanding finery of their own. Feverishly she tried to think what she could give them—

And then people were coming, men thronged into the lantern light. Father was beside her, shoving the Indians back curtly, ordering them off.

Weakly, Torrie folded up onto the steps of the tailgate. She was aware of a struggle going on, but there were more white men than redskins and soberer too. It wasn't really a serious fight.

Liza was bending over her now. "What happened? Are you hurt?"

But Torrie was shivering with a nervous sort of laughter

and couldn't tell her. Because it really was funny—the Indian going off draped in her runaway clothes. The laughter was getting away from her.

Jess was trying to explain. "She wanted to get the quilt away from them for some reason—"

"The quilt?"

"Yes. I couldn't see why she should be so upset about a plain cotton comforter."

Father had come to join them now. "A quilt!" He shook Torrie gently. "Stop it, child, stop it. Was it *the* quilt?"

Torrie nodded helplessly.

"Get hold of yourself, Victoria." Father spoke a little more sharply. "Tell us, where is it? What happened to it?"

"Underneath," she gasped, her laughter coming almost in sobs. "I threw it—under the wagon."

Liza held the lantern and Father got down to look, while the other men and Jess stood puzzled. After a minute, Thomas straightened up slowly.

"It's not there. There's nothing under the wagon but Jess's bedroll."

That jolted Torrie out of her hysteria. "But I threw it there!"

Liza turned wearily to explain to the others. "That quilt's got all our money sewed inside—every cent of our savings."

For a long awkward moment they stood there, staring at each other. And then, from within the wagon came a small stirring that made Father turn quickly. Taking the lantern from Liza, he held it up so they could all see. . . .

It was Caleb crouched far back in the corner by the stove. Under his arm was the quilt, all in a scrambled-up bundle. Clenched in his hand was the Colt revolver.

Instinctively, the men scattered aside as Father said quietly, "The danger's over, son."

Cal laid the gun down with a coolness that was slightly self-conscious. He said, "Well, I saw where she threw it and I thought somebody might get it, and no stinking old Indian is going to steal our money while I'm around."

Turning to Jess and including Torrie, Father said gravely, "I'm obliged to you both. You've saved us a serious loss." And then he added, "I'm afraid Caleb has yet to learn what it is to have courage without a gun in his hand."

JULY

WHEN THEY had left Laramie, the trains had strung out up the steepening land in one long lurching straining stumbling procession. But as they began to feel the harshness of the uphill pull, the stress began to tell on the weaker outfits. Day by day, the bluffs that had flanked them all along the valley of the Platte gave way to mountains on one side, a maze of badlands on the other. Just the sight of the endless steep rise and fall of the trail ahead was enough to discourage the fainthearted ones. Some turned back, some just lagged and whined in indecision, and others went on desperately, hurriedly, double-teaming with somebody else when their cattle flagged from exhaustion. They pushed on, and yet hated to see the miles fall behind, for each step brought them nearer the point where they'd have to leave the Platte. For so long it had been the tenuous lifeline guiding them through this desolate waterless land that now they dreaded to strike out away from it.

There was no frivolity in the camps these nights, nor was there any co-operation. Each man's food was his own and

114

he guarded it jealously. When Liza offered their extra milk to some family with small children, the other women of the train glared at her resentfully, for they did not share with anyone. The only effort they made to work together was what was forced upon them by mutual necessity. Where one team wasn't enough to haul a wagon up a steep grade, they traded labor and oxen, but it was done in grudging suspicion, every man quick to claim that his own oxen were being used too hard.

Their desperation came through in even rawer patches once they left the Platte and headed out across the alkali plateau. It was hard to believe that these were the people who had danced together at Laramie only two weeks ago. And yet, the sights that were strewn along the trail were enough to frighten anyone. Dead oxen every mile or so, their bones picked by last night's coyotes and wolves. Wagons broken down and abandoned—most of them were the new ones that Torrie had admired so in Independence. The gay-colored canvas tops were faded now, she could hardly read the lettering: *54-40 or Fight*. She wondered if it could be the same schooner that had stood so handsome and smelled so pleasantly of fresh carpentry two months ago. The green wood had dried now, warping and splitting; the wheels had shrunk to where the spokes were falling out and the iron tires had come off. It made her think of what Grandpa had said about this sturdy old wagon of theirs that creaked onward so steadily. Age can improve wood, and applejack—and people. Some people.

Not many of the emigrants seemed to have strengthened under these last months, she thought. Most of them seemed to be going to pieces—they didn't even keep their clothes clean and mended, but shoved on fearfully, their tatters flapping. When they stopped at night, they couldn't seem to settle for a few hours' rest, but bickered with each other and gulped their food hastily, doling out the small rations of water and lashing out at the children when they cried for more.

All along the trail, stranded families hurled foul epithets at the ones who drove on unheeding of their pleas for charity. Liza always managed to give the people with children a little of her own dwindling stock of food, but she couldn't feed everybody who needed it.

The salt pork in the crocks was almost gone now, and there hadn't been any money to replenish the supply—not at the prices that had been asked at Laramie. That was the trouble with almost everybody—they hadn't been able to afford much food and now the buffalo weren't so plentiful either. The wagons that had traveled the trail ahead of them had hunted so often and long that other game had scattered and grown wary. Sometimes after a whole day of hunting Father came back with only a few birds, although he was turning out to be a better shot than most of the men. For a few days, they ate plentifully of a new kind of fowl that Torrie hadn't tasted before, a chicken-like bird that fed off the sage so that the meat was strong with sage flavor. But as the country became drier and more alkaline, there simply was no game at all to be found.

This really put people into a blind lethargy of fear. Their dried foods almost exhausted, whole families came down sick, either from the insufficient diet or the mountain fever that came on in the higher elevations. If it hadn't been for the milk, Torrie thought, they would have suffered more themselves. As it was, she got a touch of dizziness sometimes, but a drink of fresh milk usually drove it off. Liza

116

felt the altitude severely and was forced to take to her bed, but Father and Cal seemed unaffected by it. And Jess— whatever he felt, nobody knew. He just walked along doggedly, day after day, coaxing and badgering and lar- ruping the oxen up the long grade, seeing to it that they followed the easiest way possible, and tending to their needs at night with the grim intentness of a doctor.

So far, the original stock was holding up well; the ones they had bought in Independence were far weaker. They kept the two extra animals close to their own wagon these days, with Cal posted as guard against possible thievery, but the real difficulty was lack of forage and the oxen were gaunting badly. Jess allowed a guess that this team had been shipped in from some other part of the country and weren't too strong to start with. Whatever it was, it seemed to be the case with a good many of the cattle that had been bought in Independence, and whenever a family had to unhitch a dying ox, and go on with a smaller team, it meant they also had to leave some of their load behind. A pitiful collection of valuables lay strewn all along the back trail—furniture, tools, cartons of extra clothes, trunks and cooking utensils, even heavy family silverware. And nobody following after was willing to stop long enough to pick up any of it and add to their own heavy loads. It just made them whip their oxen to go faster.

"Get on past," Jess would mutter, as some impatient teamster would yell at him to move aside. "Go on, I'll see you later, friend." And he would lead the team over and let them blow while the other outfit went plowing past. More than once, his warning had proven true and they had passed the same wagon, a day later, broken down and helpless, with only two or three oxen left, while the whole family stood around fighting over what must be left behind.

Because of this madness coming upon them, the emigrants hardly ever kept to the same train two days in a row. Some outfits pulled on ahead, others lagged behind. There were times when Torrie wasn't sure what train they were with. But always, at nightfall, Jess saw to it that they formed up in some corral with the outfit that happened to be nearest them. And for all that he was young among the other men, he made sure that nobody took unfair advantage of them or used the Anders teams without fair return of help.

In fact, Torrie was beginning to wonder what they would have done without Jess.

II

In a tattered tent, out under the blazing hot afternoon sun, with the white dust of the trail traffic sifting in through the torn places, everything was still at last and the women around the cot straightened up wearily. From outside came the shout and hubbub of wagons going on past, but, within the tent, there was a tired silent satisfaction. Even the harassing envies and suspicions were forgotten in the age-old awe and kinship of women in the presence of birth.

It was the first time Torrie had ever seen a "bornin'," as the older women called it. It had seemed terrifying at first, and then at the end, everything had happened so fast—the baby was there, it cried a little, but not very loud or long. Now the tired mother on the bed held it in her arms, staring down at it anxiously. It was a thin baby, not so pink as Torrie thought it should have been.

"You reckon he'll be all right?" The woman looked up at them wearily.

"Sure and it's a boy then," one of the others reassured her. "Boys make strong babies."

Liza said, "I'll bring you some milk, Mrs. Peggs. That's all that's wrong, you should have been drinking more milk, and when we reach water, we'll stop and wait for you so's you can have milk regular for a while." She packed the spirits of camphor back into her little medicine bag.

One of the others moved over to ask her, "You got any laudanum in there, Missus? Enough to spare me a little?"

Liza hesitated. "I don't have much."

"Ours all got used up when our boy died, back on the Platte. Foot smashed under a wagon wheel and the gangrene set in. Eight years old—" The woman spoke with a leaden tonelessness, as if to hide the trembling inner sorrow that still swelled up at the memory.

Liza dug down in her bag. "You have a bottle to put some in?"

Torrie lifted the flap of the tent and walked out into the sun. Even the hot dust haze was a relief after the closeness in there, the sight of the silent painful struggle of the birth. Unsteadily she walked back to their own wagon. One more life to make up for a boy lying dead back in some unmarked grave in the willows beside the Platte. . . .

Father saw her now and got up from the shade of the wagon to come across to her. Like all of them, he was showing the strain of this terrible stretch of alkali—his face was almost black with the burn of the dust and his eyes were swollen and red. And yet the calmness still was in command.

"Is it finished?" he asked. "Did the child live?"

Torrie nodded.

"Will your mother be coming soon?" He tried not to

119

sound urgent, but then there was no time to allow for much delay. Not only was he anxious to catch Hastings before that train left for California, but they were perilously close to being out of water. They had carried all they could when they'd left the last spring, but it was almost gone, there was hardly enough for the cattle tonight, and no end to this poisonous land in sight.

"Mother will be along," Torrie said woodenly. "She wants to leave them some milk. I'll get it."

The Guernsey was beginning to look gaunt, like the rest of the stock, and the amount she gave each day had dwindled perceptibly. Torrie set the stool in place and went to work, her fingers accomplishing mechanically what they had fumbled over a few months before. But she was past thinking about all the little hectic things that used to seem important and troublesome. They'd all faded under the harsh burden of the sun, the corrosive dryness and no water. . . .

And suddenly the whole fear that was infecting the rest of the emigrants—the terror of defeat—swarmed over her like a sickness. How could anybody make it? Across a treacherous unyielding endless country like this where babies were born pale and emaciated, and little boys died without a doctor, without enough laudanum to dull their torment. And no end to it—no end to it—

"Torrie!" Her mother was bending over her, shaking her by the shoulder. "Torrie, what is it? What's the matter? Are you sick?"

She looked up through the tears that were streaming down her face and shook her head wordlessly.

Father had come over too, but he didn't ask questions. He said, "Go on and finish the milking, Liza, I'll take care of her." With a firm hand on her arm, he led Torrie away from the wagon and the tent and the trail over to some rocks, beyond which was nothing but the shimmering hot land, buckled up and eaten away into a labyrinth of tortured hills. Through the blur of her tears, Torrie looked at them and the fear twisted her tighter inside.

Seating her on a rock, Father sat down beside her and put an arm around her shoulders. It was such an unusual gesture for him to make that, even as she surrendered to it and clung to him, Torrie felt shy, as if this were some kind stranger who had come to sit beside her. He didn't say anything—his quiet acceptance of her mood steadied Torrie better than any words could have. When she looked up at him, there was a sympathy in his eyes so full of understanding she didn't even try to explain what had come over her.

"It happens to all of us at one time or another," he said. "To witness the distress of others is harder than bearing your own. I've always thought women were most fortunate, though. They have the release of tears. Men have to search for other outlets."

It came back to Torrie how he had sat that whole terrible day on the Platte with the book in his hands.

"The poetry?" she asked, dabbing at her eyes.

"Poetry? No, that's a stimulant. That's more useful when your own personal distress threatens to engulf your powers of reason. Why should you think of that just now?"

A little ashamed, she said, "I'm afraid it was my own distress that was bothering me."

"Well, then, the poetry might help." He smiled a little. "At least I find it puts a miraculous stiffening in me."

"How?" she wondered. "How does that poem about

the cow make you feel better?"

"The cow?"

"You know—'Forth, beast, out of thy stall.' "

"Oh. Yes. Yes." His face took on an old serenity. "That's a wonderful few lines, but don't take the 'beast' too literally. It only likens the unimaginative man to a stabled animal. The key to the thought is in the words around it:

"Forth, pilgrim, forth! Forth, beast, out of thy stall!
Know thy country. Look up. Thank God of all.
Hold the high way and let thy spirit lead.
Truth shall deliver thee; there's naught to dread."

The ring of the words worked a curious relief upon Torrie. The hills out there seemed somehow less terrifying. Only deadly if you ran headlong into their wilderness. Hold the high way—that was what they were doing. And they were certainly going to know their country!

Somewhere over on the trail, a driver yelled an obscenity at his cattle; his voice was strident with that desperation that she herself had just now felt.

"Poor devil," Father murmured. "His brute instinct has submerged his higher resources. There he is, a creature given the power to think and reason, and he's thrown it over in animal panic, stampeded by superstitious fears of the unknown ahead, instead of trusting his spirit to lead him through safely. There are many motives which prompt men to move along this trail, Victoria, but not all of them are stout enough reasons to bolster a man who has not learned to think. Dread is a poison more deadly than this alkali—it corrodes some irreplaceable fiber that holds a man upright."

Remembering her own inner stampede, Torrie said,

subdued, "I'm sorry I let go just now."

"I'm not," Thomas told her cheerfully. "I've thought it was coming for quite a while. You've changed a good deal, my child, since the day we spent alone down on the Platte. You've probably come to realize, maturely, just what we're up against, and now that you've faced it, you'll be all right. I'm glad, because the days ahead may be our most difficult." He stood up, and she realized that while he had been talking he had also been watching westward. "Here's Jess," he said. "I sent him on ahead to see if there's any sign of water to be reached tomorrow."

The Virginian rode up fast on the mare, saw them standing apart, and headed straight over to them. As he slid down from the heaving horse, he nodded.

"We're coming out onto the river they told of . . . must be . . . the Sweetwater. . . ." Short of breath from his ride, he took a long gulp of air. "Country's opening out ahead . . . it's green . . . looks like easy going up the river. And big. . . ." He looked at Torrie now, his eyes full of the farness he had seen ahead of them. "I never saw anything so big in my life."

III

The trip up the Sweetwater gave them back some of their failing energies. Grass was deep along the borders of the sinuous stream, and on every side the dry sageland was creased by little furrows of greenery where springs had freshened the earth. Even the peaks that they glimpsed ahead to the northwest, rising higher every day, were forested and verdant. There were still pockets of last winter's snow on the awesome ragged heights of these

Wind River Mountains—the most towering Torrie had ever seen.

Game was suddenly abundant; the antelope raced off too fast to draw a good bead on, but there were scattered herds of buffalo along the broad valley and, on the higher slopes that led off toward the mountains, deer and wild fowl. What with fresh food and a bounty of good clear cold water again, the travelers began to show a little reviving spirit beneath the haggard masks of their faces.

But they kept moving. The nights were getting cooler and the swift little thunderstorms that showered down off the mountains brought a chill that made them feel the season turning. The long grade was gentle most of the time, and the cattle were beginning to pick up weight and step out more strongly. It gave Torrie a new sort of pleasure to feel the thrust of the big beasts leaning into the yoke, drawing them up into the heart of this untouched country. With a quickening of secret pride, she liked to think of how few white women had ever seen this land, magnificent in its vastness. As Jess had said, it was big beyond belief.

She was beginning to know Jess a little better. Up to now, there had been so little time free of the tasks of the journey. But now sometimes when they reached a stretch of particularly level ground, he would swing up into the seat of the front wagon. An occasional sharp command kept the oxen going right along, while he delved into Cal's old speller and puzzled over the words.

It seemed to do him more good than a night's sleep, to dig into that book. He got so lost in contemplation of the lessons that Torrie marveled at it. She was careful not to let on that she considered it the least unusual, though. Since his secret had been forced out into the open, Jess was a good deal less defiant of her, but her intuition told her it wouldn't take much to put him on the defensive again.

She could understand that he might have felt resentful at first, knowing that she had all the schooling he didn't have, but she honestly couldn't help wondering why it was so important to him—what made him hunger so for the words in the fraying little red book. Sometimes he'd skip to the back and puzzle over the fourth- and fifth-grade lists. There were times when Torrie wished keenly that she could help him, but some hunch told her to wait until he asked. And then one day he did.

They were alone up on the front seat of the wagon. As usual, Cal was off somewhere on the buckskin, which Jess had let him use freely ever since they had left Fort Laramie. Father had bought a saddle for only a few dollars from a family who needed to lighten their load, and now, daily, Cal galloped off, the old Boone rifle in hand, chasing every flock of antelope or covey of sage chicken in his path. He was getting to be a fair shot and an even better rider.

Liza was still feeling the altitude, but she was able to be up some of the time and spent most of it back in the Peggses' wagon which followed along just behind. It was plainly a pleasure for her to help care for the new baby.

As for Father, finding the demands upon him relaxed briefly, he spent the days drifting ahead or back down the trail to talk to the other men. The issue looming large for all of them was whether or not to take the Hastings cutoff.

And so it was that Torrie found herself alone with Jess that day. He'd given her the whip to hold while he paged through the speller, clear to the back of the book. Suddenly his head came up, the blond thatch of hair falling loose over

125

his eyes. Impatiently he slicked it back.

"Look here, Torrie, I found a humdinger." He frowned. "What does t-h-o-u-g-h-t spell?"

"That's 'thought,'" she told him.

"All those letters for such a short word?" He shook his head. "I don't understand it." For a while he studied the word, and then sat back and spelled it silently to the sky. "I think I've got it—that's an important one, too. Must have put those extra letters in to make it look worthwhile."

"How do you mean, important?" she asked curiously. He seemed so much more at ease with her than usual, it was a temptation to find out just what was going on behind those deep-set eyes. Searching eyes, a lot like Grandpa's. . . .

Jess had closed the book and was holding it balanced in his hand as if it were a palmful of silver. "These words—they're all important but some more than others. They're the ones that make the difference. You don't know because you never sat around the farmhouse night after night, listening to your pa and your brothers and uncles and aunts, all gabbling about nothing—who they saw at the store and what he was buying and who he'd come with and what they'd talked about—more nothing. On and on, like a flock of geese. It wasn't hardly human. No t-h-o-u-g-h-t." He smiled as if at some private joke that wasn't very funny.

"Is that why you ran away?" she ventured.

"I didn't run away, I came away and nobody cared. I rode up first to the Capitol—I thought I'd like to see the government. Do you know that anybody can walk right in and see the Senate? And that's where I heard talking like never before." Jess looked at her with a quickened excitement, his shyness forgotten. "That was really something!

126

The words they used—it was Thomas Hart Benton and another man named John Calhoun, and when they sat down there were others. All talking about California and Oregon and what this country is going to be some day." He shook his head at the memory. "I never heard the like. I couldn't understand half of it." Fiercely he shook the speller under her nose. "I just had to find out, don't you see? What good are you if you can't understand men like that?"

"But why did you come west? You could have stayed in the east and got better schooling."

Jess looked at her startled, coming out of his inner vision to find that he had just spoken aloud a lot of things he'd evidently intended to keep bottled up inside. Somewhat embarrassed, he took the whip and made a little concern over popping a deer fly off the neck of the lead ox, did it so neatly the animal didn't even notice.

At last he said, "I've got no money, for schooling or anything else. Back east, everything's used up. If you want land, you got to pay high for it. If you work for somebody, you just make enough to get by on. Most folks around home were in debt. That's not for me. I want to pay my bills as I go. And make my work count. All I need is a chance—there's a lot of room out here, ought to be enough for a man to get a few acres cheap, maybe even free if California gets taken into the States. Give me a little land and I'll show you—I'll have a good farm in three years and a good herd in ten. Meantime your pa's going to teach me, when we both get time. Money won't do me any good if I can't stand up and speak my piece with other men. I want to have a say-so in my county some day, I reckon my ideas are as good as anybody's if I could just form 'em into words. That's why words are important. You think I'm crazy?" He demanded it abruptly, turning to pin her down with a hard-eyed stare that she couldn't look away from.

"No," she blurted swiftly, "I think it's wonderful. I wish I knew what I wanted to do. I wish I wanted something that badly—"

"You've got a man like your father to help you figure things, and you don't know?" He spoke almost angrily.

"Father never tells anybody what to be or do."

"Maybe not, but just living around him ought to firm up your ideas. I'd have given my right arm to grow up around a man with all that sense."

"Well—sense—" Torrie was honestly perplexed. "He's —he's very smart, I know, especially about poetry and all—"

"Poetry!" Jess exploded. "I'm not talking poetry. He's got brains and school learning to go with 'em and gumption to back 'em up. You act like you don't know your own pa. Don't you ever listen to him?"

Torrie had to admit inwardly that for a long time, back home, she hadn't. His talk always seemed so far removed from the little day-by-day events that interested her. But then, this was what Jess had run away from, that kind of gossip. He'd given her another side of the picture.

"I'm just beginning to know Father," she said. "This trip —I never dreamed he could do the things he's done."

"Then you're too close to the woods to see the trees," Jess told her flatly. "I knew the minute I heard him talking to the outfitter there in Independence. Your pa wasn't going to be fleeced. He was polite about it, but the outfitter got called a thief in the plainest way. I knew then that your pa was a positive man, he wasn't going to go to pieces first

128

time something rough came along. I followed him around that whole day, just listening, and then I looked your wagon over and it looked sound. I figured this outfit would get to California. That's why I asked to hire on." He glanced at her sideways. "Or did you think it was just because your pa had a beautiful daughter?"

Torrie felt herself go painfully warm. She looked down at her folded hands intently. There had been times when she wouldn't have minded so much being teased on her looks, and other people who could have done it, but just now—from Jess—

"Wait now," he said hurriedly, "you didn't take me wrong, did you? I meant no smartness by that."

"I know," she said wistfully. "It's just me. I hate being so plain. I wish I *were* beautiful."

"You wish what? Look here—" Jess touched her arm lightly to make her turn toward him. As she raised her look to meet his, he was searching her face as if it puzzled him. "You meant it!" he spoke in amazement. "You really think you're—what did you call it? Plain?"

"Oh, I know I'm not pretty." She tried to laugh, but it wouldn't work.

"No, you're not pretty." His tone had gentled almost unbelievably. "But don't you know that you've got—" He broke off. "I'd better not tell you, might go to your head."

Torrie smiled in spite of herself. He was being nice, of course. There was no other explanation. Trying to hint that she was attractive, to keep her from feeling bad. It was even heart-warming that he should want to shield her from the truth. With a small humor, she said, "Don't worry. I look in the mirror every morning. I'm not likely to get conceited, no matter what you say."

Jess stood up, ready to swing down out of the wagon and take the trail again. "Don't bother with mirrors," he said, strangely serious. "But if you really want to know whether I was fooling you, one of these days—say, two or three years from now—look at yourself in a man's eyes."

And now the talk along the train was all of crossing the Continental Divide. Torrie had been worrying about it ever since they'd left St. Louis, trying to picture it: something like the peak of a roof, with the land rising to a sharp ridge on one side of which the water rushed away toward the east and, on the other, flowing westward. It must almost *have* to be the worst part of the trip, climbing the top of the continent.

So it was that on the morning when they crossed the Sweetwater for the last time and the trail took off overland, she told Jess anxiously, "You'd better be ready for a steep pull today. Everybody says we'll be crossing the Divide."

He frowned and scanned the country ahead, but the broad grasslands stretched away, level as an avenue between the mountains off to the north and the towering string of buttes that rose sheer on the southwest, like the portals of a gateway. "I don't see anything bad ahead unless we climb those consarned cliffs," he said, halfway mocking, but still a little puzzled himself, Torrie thought.

By noon, there still hadn't appeared any barrier except the natural wrinkles of the prairie land. When Thomas rode up beside them, they looked to him for the answer.

"The Divide?" he repeated. "Why, very likely we're upon it right now. Come to think of it, I believe I've felt the land tilting a different way—"

"So have I," admitted Jess. "At least we've been going downhill more than we've gone up, this last hour."

And that was all there was to it. Jess couldn't help teasing Torrie all that afternoon. She didn't hesitate to josh him right back, but secretly she was tasting the anticipation of their new home more sharply than ever before. And when they stopped at the first spring, she got down from the wagon and cupped some of the water in her hands, burying her face in its ice-cold freshness.

"Just think," she called to Jess. "This water's bound for the Pacific Ocean. It's California water!"

"Taste different?" Jess asked with one of those slow smiles.

She started to answer him tartly, then, on a different impulse, she went over to the wagon, took down the dipper, and brought him some. "It's not like St. Louis water," she said, and she meant it.

The Virginian drank gratefully, then handed the dipper back, looking down at her with the humor gone and a softness in his eyes. "I reckon that's what women are for," he said, "to make dreams out of plain stuff like water. Thank you, it tasted good, all right."

It was a relief to be on a downhill grade, and the time seemed to run faster after that. The realness of California loomed larger all the while, especially when, a day later, they reached the sage flat where the trail divided again, as it had before, just outside of Independence, only this time the Anders family took the south arm while most of the wagons veered north, bound for Oregon. There was a good deal of leave-taking, and some of the women who weren't even very good friends cried and carried on in a way that made Liza shake her head at their silliness. And

131

yet it did seem strange to see so many of the people they had traveled with heading off along a different trail.

The Peggs family had been Oregon-bound too, but at the last minute they'd changed their minds. Mr. Peggs, a helpless pudgy little man, said he'd heard too much about the rainy spells out there, but Torrie thought privately it was the Guernsey cow that was beckoning the way to California.

Of course a few others were going on to Fort Bridger, too, most of them hurrying to join Mr. Hastings' train, for the word of it had spread along the trail. And now the talk was growing more heated. There were lengthy discussions between the men who had read the Hastings book and *knew* that the cutoff was the best and shortest way, and the others who had studied the writing of an army man, a Captain Frémont, who had described the route through Soda Springs as the *only* safe way to go.

Thomas Anders hadn't made up his mind. From the little Pacific Creek, all the way down the Sandy to the Green River, across the dry eroded land to the Black's Fork, which would take them to Fort Bridger, Father kept turning the matter over, discussing it with the other men. He respected Jim Clyman's words, he said it many times. Clyman was a mountain man who had no reason to lie. And yet the saving of four hundred miles would mean, presumably, just that much extra energy for both stock and men to be spent on the last leg of the trip, down the Humboldt and across the Sierra, which was the hardest part of the whole trail. He kept hoping that by now some new way had been found to get through the mountains, some route that might have been discovered since Clyman left to go east. At least, he couldn't make up his mind until he had talked to Hastings in person.

"I'd like to judge," he said, "whether the man is a conscientious sort or merely some opportunist trying to lure people with talk of an easy route, hoping to take them where he can sell them real estate."

But as they came off the dry wastes into the little valley and made their way up to the modest log stockade (this was no Laramie, this fort!), they could see at a glance that there was no sign of a battalion of wagons waiting to entrain across the mountains. In fact the valley was almost deserted. Lansford Hastings had gone on.

AUGUST

IT WAS a strange uneasy family, with Father absent from the circle. Torrie felt as if there were a huge empty gap in their wholeness. She even missed Caleb—without his hectoring the wagon seemed uncomfortably still. What with both Jess and Mother being, by nature, quiet, Torrie got to feeling as though they were all moving in a whisper.

Ever since her bout with mountain sickness, Mother had been looking tired, and now it showed more plainly than ever. She hadn't really approved of Father's decision to go on ahead and scout the mountains before taking the wagon through, even though his reasoning was perfectly sound. Father's judgment was always well thought out.

That last night before he'd left, he'd explained firmly, "There is no other sensible course. Clyman thought the short cut through the Wasatch might possibly be made by wagon; Hastings has presumably just gone through with some sixty-odd parties in his train not a week ago, according to Mr. Bridger. Bridger himself seems to think it can be done and he verifies the fact that there would be a substantial saving in actual distance. With the season getting later and the oxen more weary, every mile counts. If the difficulties are surmountable, I'm inclined to chance the crossing. However, once we're embarked upon that course, there'll be no turning back. If we go straight on into the Wasatch with the wagon and find they are impassable, it will be too late to come all the way back here and make a new start along the northern route. That's why it seems inevitable that I go ahead and see at firsthand what we're up against. From what Bridger tells me, I can probably make it through the mountains on horseback in three days and return in the same time. Then we'll know for certain what the elements of our decision are."

It was so like Father—you'd have thought he was giving a lecture on the foundations of Shakespearean drama or something, Torrie thought. Sometimes his deliberation was exasperating—it always made so much sense. Mother had accepted it, but she hadn't been happy.

And so he had packed his saddlebags, and, at the last minute, Caleb had turned up with his own saddle on the buckskin and demanded so fiercely to be allowed to go that it became a point of manhood against childhood, and there was no answer for it but to say "yes." In the face of his urgency, even Mother hadn't put up much objection.

But after they had ridden out across the meadows toward the western ridges that led to the mountains, she had gone about her chores too briskly, throwing herself into work that didn't really need to be done, deliberately exhausting herself, Torrie thought. And all those next days, when she wasn't helping Mrs. Peggs, Liza was busy over the stove. The tart wild cherries were just coming ripe along the creek bottom, and she busied herself with making preserves

135

and syrup, using what little sugar they could spare, drying the rest of the cherries like raisins. Busy . . . busy . . . too busy to think.

One thing was fortunate. Mr. Bridger could assure them that no Mormons had come this way yet, although this was the part of the West that they were heading for. Even though Father said that they were just plain people, Torrie had heard the awful tales people were telling of them and she was glad he'd have neither them nor the Indians to worry about. All in all, she was enjoying this stay in Bridger's valley.

The wagon was pulled up not far from the fort under the shade of a big cottonwood tree, and after the long hot trip down the Black's Fork, the coolness was an acute relief. To be free from dust for a while, free of the motion of the trail and the scream of dry axles, even a fair supply of field hay for the cattle—Torrie thought it would be good just to stay here forever.

She liked the brittle clearness of the air. At night when the sky cooled down to blue-black, the stars were flung across its bottomless depths more brilliant than she had ever seen them. Their thick clustering looked so near above, she wanted to reach out to them—full of some nameless hunger that made her ache inside, some new awareness that needed to be shared.

As if he felt it too, Jess came to her one evening, came slowly but purposefully over as though he'd been holding off and now was giving in to the same need. He'd been working so hard these days, doing both his own chores and Cal's, seeing to the stock, digging at his books, they had hardly had much talk together. Now he leaned back beside her against a low branch of the tree and they looked together at the stars strewn broadcast overhead.

"I wish I knew how to read 'em," he said distantly. "The old men know. Star signs are like handwriting to them. I heard old Bridger today when I was at the Fort. He said it's coming on to be an early winter. How did he know? How do you learn things like that?"

Torrie was silent, thinking of Grandpa—how he always knew when to put seed into the ground. How his hands went so smoothly about the business of making a neat splice in a piece of broken harness. She thought of how her mother made bread, folding it and kneading it just one more time and then once more, and it was ready to set to rise. She never could say just why or how she knew when it was done. And of course there was Father's own peculiar inner kind of calculation—whatever it was that had made him come on this trip. She still wondered about that, more and more as its hardships unfolded. What he had told them down on the Platte, about finding out their capacities, was part of it. But there was still some secret reason—she couldn't say why but she was sure of it.

It occurred to Torrie what a tremendous decision it must have been to Jess—to make up his own mind to journey all this way alone.

"How old are you, Jess?" she asked, before she'd thought how bold it might sound to him.

He took it as a reasonable question. "Seventeen," he said.

That shocked Torrie out of her dreaminess. "But you're—! I mean, I thought you were older!"

He was silent a minute; in the darkness she couldn't see his expression. At last, he said, "You disappointed?"

"No!" she retorted, almost too emphatically. "I was just

surprised. You're only two years older than I am. At least, I'll be fifteen—" And then she stopped short, amazed. "Why, I'll be fifteen on August the second. How soon do you figure that is?" Because she had long since lost track of the days.

"Today was the first," he told her quietly.

For a minute, the thought of the birthday overwhelmed her, with all that it implied. And then the other significance of what he'd said got home to her and she turned to him, dismayed.

"But Father said he'd be back before the first!"

"I know."

"That means he's been gone—"

"Seven days."

"Does Mother—do you think she's been keeping count?"

"Of course she has."

Torrie fell silent, ashamed of herself for having been so unaware of the time passing here in this timeless little valley. It seemed as if Father had been gone for a long long while, and yet, as if he'd barely ridden away over the hill.

"I guess it was farther than he thought across the mountains," she faltered. But he'd only taken food for a week. "I'm glad he carried the rifle," she added.

"He wasn't of a mood to hunt," Jess said shortly. "That's why he took food with him. He knew it was important to get back fast. He meant to be here by now. I don't like it." Turning to glance around them, he added, "Look—only four campfires and one of 'em is ours. Everybody else pulled out and gone on."

Torrie had been a little uneasy about that herself, especially since the Donners had taken their big train westward yesterday. They had come in the day after Father left, with a handsome assortment of the biggest, fanciest wagons, a herd of cattle that were fine and well kept compared to most of the trail stock. They were gentlefolk, too —Mrs. Donner had been friendly and warm with Mother and had given Mrs. Peggs some paregoric for the baby, who had the colic. All in all, it had been a wonderful foretaste of what life in California was going to be. For these families were headed for the Sacramento Valley too, and they were well-favored people. Their wagons were almost luxurious and they still had all their valuables brought with them clear from Illinois, yet they weren't haughty like the Colonel and his wife. They talked a lot about Mr. Hastings' book—they'd followed it to the letter all along the trail and they had no doubt that the short cut was the very best possible route to get to the Humboldt River. They wouldn't think of going by way of Soda Springs!

Yes, they said, they'd talked to Jim Clyman too—in fact, he had stopped by their train the very evening after he'd left the Anders camp in Laramie. And wasn't he a worrier? They laughed a little, politely, and pointed out that Jim was a mountain man, at home on horseback, but he couldn't be expected to know how good a sturdy wagon is at going over rough country. Everyone in their party was sure they'd make it through the Wasatch easily, and as for the Salt Desert, well you just carry enough water. It's only a day's travel to the next spring. Oh yes, only a day's travel. Mr. Hastings' book said so. In fact, the Donners and their friends were so calmly confident that some of the people who had stopped in the valley, to wait for Thomas Anders to get back with word about the trail, decided to take a chance on the short way. They joined the Donner train—

139

the McCutcheons and the Murphys and some of the others. As Mrs. McCutcheon told Liza, it might be the last big train bound for California and it was safer to be with a large outfit.

The Donners had even urged Mother to yoke up and come with them. They were sure they'd meet Father returning along the trail, and think of the time it would save. But Liza had thanked them and gone back to her busywork.

Glancing over at Jess now, Torrie asked, "Do you think we should have gone on with the Donners yesterday?"

"Certainly not," he said. "Your pa told us to wait. We'll never get west if everybody starts outguessing each other. He's counting on us to stay here and this is where we stay. Only thing that really worries me is your ma. She's taking this harder than you know. It's up to you and me to pick up some of the slack of her misery."

"But what—?" And then Torrie had it. "I know! We'll have a birthday party for me tomorrow!"

The next day there was an intent look—a proudness— on Liza's face as she wielded the comb on Torrie's hair, stuck in a pin here and there, brushed and tucked and pinned again, then stepped back to view the results with a little smile, as if she had just discovered something.

Seizing the mirror, Torrie surveyed herself. The dark straight locks were brushed back into two loose graceful wings that ended in a soft roll at the nape of her neck. It wasn't exactly curls, but it made her look wonderfully older. It made her look—like Liza. And what bewildered her most was that she didn't mind! All at once, it was good to look like Mother.

"All these years, just because you're dark and slight, I been thinking you took after your pa entirely." Liza shook her head. "Sometime I'll show you a sketch—one of my young men was a great hand with a pen, did my picture when I was about your age. You'd be surprised." Abruptly she turned away, a little fluttery. "My land, I most forgot the cake."

Torrie watched her climb down and go to the makeshift oven they had rigged up—just an empty tin tea box set over the coals of the fire, but if anybody could bake a cake in a tea box, Torrie thought, it would be Mother. To imagine her as a young girl was to conjure up whole mysteries— was she vivacious and warm as she'd been the night she'd danced at Fort Laramie? She mentioned "one of my young men." Then she must have had beaux and chances for marriage. Which meant that she had really been in love with Father after all, and had not just married him as a last resort, as Torrie had imagined for so long. And remembering that day when Mother had confronted Colonel Carroll, Torrie thought that for Liza, at least, it had been a real romance— that it wasn't over either.

As she went about the small ritual of getting dressed, Torrie wondered about being in love—what it must be like. She'd always had some vague idea that it was a dangerous sensation, like being swept over by a wind or whirled around in a swift current of water. But you couldn't picture Mother being overcome by that sort of emotion. So then, what was it? How did it feel?

Fastening the belt of her dress, she picked up the mirror again. It was her Sunday best—a green silk—and she had always hated it. It still looked terribly demure, but the tucks that Mother had taken in the waist did improve the fit and made the bodice seem fuller. With a certain surprise, Torrie noticed that she filled the blouse out somewhat more roundly than she had four months ago when she'd last had the dress on at home.

Mother had come back now to sit in the rear opening of the wagon, looking at her still with that awakening appreciation. "You know, your color's a whole lot better than it used to be," she observed, "seems to me you put on some weight. You'll make the boys turn their heads one of these days."

Torrie thought of Luke Egan. "I'm not sure I want to," she said with a touch of bitter humor.

"I don't mean you'll need to be forward about it," Liza told her. "It'll just come natural—you won't be able to help it. And it'll be proper, too. Young fellows ought to come around when a girl gets to marrying age. That's not the same as flirting and carrying on light."

On an impulse, Torrie blundered out with the question that had been on her mind. "How did you come to marry Father?" When she'd said it, it seemed a terribly bold thing to have asked, but Liza didn't seem to mind.

"You mean how did he come to ask me?" she smiled. "I must say I don't know; I wasn't pretty, and for certain I wasn't well schooled like he is. When I see Jess digging into those books, it reminds me of how I tried to read those hard poems of your father's when we were first keeping company. But then I couldn't seem to stick to it like Jess does. Good thing your father saw somewhat else in me to want to marry."

"But how did you choose him?"

That seemed to surprise Liza. "Why, I just knew. Couldn't say how. I'd given over the idea of getting married at all. Every farm fellow I knew was all settled in to follow a plow down the same field the rest of his life. I couldn't feel stirred up over them, and the city men seemed loud and showy, I didn't trust them. So I'd just made up my mind to be a spinster, and then your father come along. He was quiet—a thinking kind of quiet—and I knew right off he was a man wouldn't ever go back on his word, I knew he'd raise good children. . . ." She hesitated, groping for words. "Oh, all that came after, though. Why I married him was something I couldn't say—I just looked at him standing there looking at me, and I knew we were meant. That's all. You'll see some time, I hope, only don't be in a hurry. Takes some looking at odd breeds before you can pick out good blood—in beasts or men."

Unconsciously Torrie repeated something that Jess had said. "But how do you ever learn to know things like that?"

Her mother smiled. "Don't worry. It's a kind of sense that grows on you." Then she added, "That cake's about done. Let's go find where Jess has got to."

They discovered the Virginian out behind the big tree, bent in frowning concentration before a scrap of mirror that he'd got somewhere. Intently he was trying to crop the lanky blond hair.

"My goodness, so that's what you wanted the scissors for!" Liza laughed fondly and sat him down on a packing box they'd set out there as a table. "Here, let me do it. Nobody can cut his own hair right." He had washed the tow-colored thatch in the stream, and it shone like a horses's mane under the sun. "Now hold still!" she admonished him sharply—Jess had just caught sight of Torrie.

In a sort of awe, he sat and looked at her while she smiled at the amazement in his eyes. And then, all at once, it went beyond smiling and there was some wordless interchange between them. Just as he had once said—she saw herself written in the expression of his face, and his look was telling her what no mirror ever would. Even if it was only for this minute in all her life, Torrie was beautiful.

They set the cake on a tablecloth which Mother had spread on the packing crate and brought out the pot of tea, which was Jess's treat, bought from the store at the Fort. The late afternoon shadows were stretching in from the hills to the west, as Mother suggested that somebody go and tell the neighbors the party was ready. But just then, abruptly, plump little Mr. Peggs came hustling around the wagon, puffing and frowning.

"Miz Anders," he panted, "your mister's on his way in. We just sighted him comin' down the meadows. Only I don't see the boy—"

"Thomas! Alone!" Liza gathered her skirts and ran past him with Torrie and Jess close behind. What they saw made their hearts turn over. The lonely horseman was riding in slowly, they could see now that he carried a bulky huddle of blankets across the front of the saddle. The riderless buckskin limped behind on a lead rope.

Anders looked exhausted to the core as he reined in before the little group, which now included most of the other emigrants who had run over from the nearby wagons. His clothes were torn, his face streaked with dirt. For a minute, he seemed unable to find words. Liza was almost equally paralyzed, staring painfully at the burden in his arms. Torrie clung to her, whether for her own support or her mother's, it would have been hard to say.

144

Jess collected himself first, moved forward to Father's side.

"Easy." Thomas spoke hoarsely. "Cal's been hurt. Horse fell—caught his leg under it—" Stiffly he dismounted, trying to hold the bundled-up figure carefully, but as he came down, his knees almost buckled and Jess had to help him. It brought a small convulsed groan from the blankets.

"Let me take him," Jess insisted. "You're worn out, sir." He lifted the boy from Father's arms as deftly as a nurse and carried him to the wagon, Thomas stumbling along behind.

"Must keep him warm—he's in a—state of reaction—" Father still was too dazed with weariness to speak coherently. Liza was already ahead of them, turning down the quilts, making the bed ready. The others were closing in now to help; one man took the two horses and led them down toward the stream. Another offered to go get his bottle of rye whiskey.

"Thank you." Father bowed a little mechanically. "But the boys needs a stimulant—some coffee or—tea—"

"Yes," said the man, "only I was thinkin' of yourself, sir."

Torrie had already rushed to get the teapot where they'd left it on the picnic cloth.

Under his suntan, Cal was unearthly white; the waxy lifeless pallor made his freckles stand out dark and unnatural by contrast. His eyes were unfocused at first, but when they'd got some hot tea down him he began to revive. Jess, who seemed to me more knowledgeable about these matters than any of them, kept rubbing the boy's hands and wrists until a little blood came into the stricken young face.

145

Father was getting some of his strength back too, although his hands trembled noticeably when he lifted the cup of tea. He sat on the tailgate of the wagon, where he could watch as they worked over Cal and still answer the questions of the people grouped outside.

"Yes," he said, "we followed Hastings part of the way—it was a hard climb into the mountains, but a good supply of water all the way. Once in the mountains, however, he took his party into a canyon that—" He shook his head, helplessly. "I'd have said it was completely impassable. And yet—he entered it at least—left a rubble of broken wagons. I could see where they'd had to carve a trail out of the steep slope of the canyon walls in places, where the stream bed is choked with boulders and underbrush. They must have hauled the wagons up by block and tackle. I dread to think what that trip must have cost in human suffering—" His voice faded, leaving an uneasy silence.

Somebody spoke. "But they got through?"

"I don't know." Thomas shrugged. "We didn't follow them down the canyon. I knew I'd not take my wagon on such a route with or without the assistance of Mr. Hastings. So Cal and I traveled up another ravine that looked reasonably passable—the mountains are a mass of tortuous little canyons. We had to hack our way through thickets of scrub oak—again, it would have meant blazing a new trail to get a wagon across. Worse—far worse than I ever dreamed. The effort would be so time-consuming, it would more than wipe out any saving in miles, and our energies would be shattered by the prodigious effort. Even on horseback, it took us a full three days to come out upon the west face of the mountains, where several streams seemed to lead down to the plains beyond. Any of the descents would be

146

precipitous, even ruinous. And beyond we could see the Salt Lake—a vast body—it would have to be skirted circuitously. We saw no sign of wagons down there, so presumed that Hastings and his train must still be toiling down the canyons."

"What of the desert?"

"We couldn't take the time to continue on to its edge. I considered the situation as carefully as I could and came to the conclusion that Mr. Hastings is a black villain of a merchant who has sold some innocents a deceitful bill of goods, probably to their ultimate destruction. The only thing left to do was to get back as quickly as possible. And then it was that Caleb's horse slipped on one of the loose rocky slopes. That was early yesterday. Ever since, I've been in the saddle. I knew it would be a slow trip with the boy injured, and yet it was necessary to get back immediately."

"Did you pass that party left here day before yesterday? They was headin' the way you just come."

"I did," Thomas answered, with some effort. "I told their leader, Mr. Donner, just what he could expect. But I'm afraid Hastings' prose was more powerful. They went on, God help them!"

Mr. Peggs asked timidly, "Then we're going by the north route?"

"I am," said Thomas, "and it means we must leave as soon as possible. If any of you care to join us we'll be glad of your company."

Some of the women were craning to peer into the wagon. "Is the young'un hurt bad? Can he travel soon?"

"I'm no doctor," Anders said, "but I believe his leg is broken."

147

"Yes, sir, it is." Jess looked up from his cautious examination of the boy. He'd been feeling the bruised discolored leg gently. "Bone didn't come through the skin, but it's broke all right. Right here." He touched a spot just above Cal's ankle and the boy winced.

The people outside began to offer suggestions—put a knife under the mattress to cut the pain—rub tea leaves on his forehead—Torrie wished they'd go away. Their comments were fraying at her nerves even worse than the silent suffering in Cal's eyes. He was coming back fast now, and with sensation had come the hurt and fear that had been blunted before.

One of the men in the front ranks of watchers said flatly, "There ain't but one thing to do with a broke bone and that's cut the whole dern leg off, make a good clean end of it, else you're askin' for gangrene, takin' chances with his life. If you want, I got a good sharp butcher knife—"

Cal's face quivered and Liza went almost as pale as the boy was. A wave of nausea came over Torrie and she turned shuddering to Jess.

"No," the Virginian said. "Don't let 'em do it."

His quiet certainty seemed to steady them. Father turned to the people outside with as much courtesy as he could manage. "Thank you for your interest," he said, "but I believe we can handle this ourselves. As for entraining, we'll try to get on the trail for Soda Springs tomorrow. . . ." He had climbed down among them now and was leading them away from the wagon, leaving the women and Jess to face each other silently across the taut body of the boy.

In the stillness, the threatening word still hung—gangrene, one of the worst killers of the trail. Torrie swallowed hard as she stared at the swollen purplish leg with its telltale unevenness.

148

Liza looked at Jess pleadingly. "What makes you think this will heal?"

"I've seen it," he told her. "My younger brother snapped his shinbone falling out of a tree, doctor set it right enough. That bruise isn't harmful and the swelling just comes from the ends of the bone rubbing. What it needs is to be straightened out and a better splint put on." Thomas had braced the leg with branches bound about it, but it had necessarily been a makeshift job. "Do you want me to try to set it, ma'am?" Jess asked.

Liza hesitated and looked to Thomas who had come back now, climbing into the wagon in time to hear the offer.

"It's good of you, Jess," he started, but there was doubt in his voice.

And then, from the bed, Cal spoke weakly. "Let Jess do it. He knows how. I can tell."

Somehow Torrie was sure too. It relieved her to see Mother finally nod and Father agree. They went to work —Thomas whittled splints out of the boards of the packing box (the birthday cake lay aside now, neglected) while Mother tore the linen tablecloth into strips. As they waited for laudanum to take the edge off Cal's senses, Torrie stayed beside him, washed his face and stroked his stubbly hair. But it was Jess who seemed to lend the needed reassurance. Cal's look never left him as he put a bandage on the boy's leg just below the knee, cushioned it well with lint, doing it so carefully that the boy hardly winced. Then he made another bandage crisscrossed around the foot and ankle, leaving two long ends on either side of the foot—Torrie couldn't see what any of this had to do with the broken place in the bone.

At last, when Cal had begun to look drowsy and Father

had the splints ready, Jess notched the lower end of each board and set them in place on either side of the broken leg, bound the tops securely to the protected padding near the knee, and whittled out a rung from one of the branches to fit into the two notches just below Cal's foot.

Glancing at Thomas, he said, "Hang onto him." Then, with one steady hard pull, he straightened the leg. Cal let out a shrill yell of pain, it took both parents to hold him, but Jess didn't falter.

"Torrie," he said evenly, "while I hold this straight, take the ends of that bandage and tie 'em around the rung—that's it."

Fumbling in her haste, she wrapped the loose ribbons of linen around the crosspiece so that Cal's foot was hitched securely to the bottom of the splints.

Breathing hard, Jess sat back. "Now it can't slip crooked again. You can turn him loose." And to Cal, he said, "It shouldn't hurt so much as it did before."

Scrubbing furiously at the tears in his eyes, the boy said, "It feels fine . . . it feels real good."

Mother let out a long sigh. "Can I wrap it now?"

"Yes, ma'am," Jess said, "but not too tight. Be sure to let the blood come through, and you won't have any gangrene."

For a minute they all felt a little limp with reaction. It had been accomplished so quickly and so well. As if to prove the success of the operation, from the pillows Cal said, with faint bravado, "I'm hungry."

While they scrambled around happily to get him something, Jess eased out through the rear of the wagon and walked off into the evening. Torrie saw him go—as soon as she could, she slipped away and walked out through the cool dusk, feeling some need to follow him.

Quietly she came down to the stream and found him sitting on a log there, his head in his hands. Even in that dim light, she could see that he was shaking as hard as if he'd just been through a bad fright.

"What is it, Jess?" She came quickly to his side. "What—?"

He shook his head without looking up.

"That was a wonderful thing you did." She sat down beside him. "Jess, we're all beholden to you."

He looked at her. "Suppose it had gone wrong? Suppose I'd done him some damage? Who am I? What right did I have to go doctorin' your family? I'm just an ignorant ox skinner, only sometimes I forget it. I take too much liberty. I ought to duck my head to you—that's what we do at home when a lady comes by. I ought to call you 'Miss'—" He came to his feet angrily. "I got no right to sit with you or walk with you or even to look at you." Turning, he walked away fast downstream.

And this time, Torrie didn't follow him. She was too stunned. For a long while, she sat absorbing the real meaning that underlay those bitter words.

II

"Tom Anders!" A voice called low outside the wagon that next morning.

Father, half-dressed, went to look out the back flap—there was something familiar about that voice. . . .

"Beckwith!" he exclaimed sharply. "By heaven! When did you get here?"

"Late last night. We've been pushing, traveling late. We've just heard here in camp that you're taking a train north today. We'd be grateful to join you."

And that was the real beginning of the Anders train. The evening before, there'd been no discussion of leadership; it had seemed to be a simple business of four wagons getting ready to take the trail together. Now, under a sky that was ominously gray, another group was asking to join—the remnants of their first traveling company, the Colonel's old train. Bunched together outside, they stood chilly and diffident, wanting Thomas to lead them.

Quickly throwing a warm shawl around her shoulders, Liza went out to where Jess was getting the campfire going. With the last of their supply, she made coffee while the others stood around the fire and told of their trials.

The Colonel and his wife had turned back for Independence somewhere along the Platte, leaving them without a leader. Mr. Beckwith had tried to take over, but everyone was still arguing and fighting, he said, refusing to do a proper share of the work. Just as Father had predicted, they all came down sick from bad sanitation and unclean camp habits. They wouldn't listen to reason, but just wanted to keep switching leaders. Mr. Duncan had been elected, but, across the alkali flats beyond the Platte, they'd gone to pieces, just as so many others had—dissensions, hysterics, finally utter disintegration with some of them rushing ahead and others falling back until nobody knew whether they were in a train or on some long treadmill with a thousand other people. Worst of all, their bickering had cost them much time. They'd been afraid they wouldn't even make Fort Bridger by August. Only in the latter days along the Sweetwater had they managed any semblance of unity, and now, faced with the final arduous part of the trip, they were turning like frightened sheep to the one man they knew had the conviction and courage to get them through to California. They said it bluntly and they meant it.

Thomas thought the matter over unhappily. "I've no wish for the job," he said at last, "but it's plain that with so many in the train we'll need some sort of organization if we hope to make up the time we've lost. If I accept the captaincy, though, it will be upon the condition of absolute co-operation from every man of you—your wives, your children, and your drivers."

"You lay out the plan, sir, and we'll do our part," Mr. Beckwith assured him humbly.

"I'll even write it down," said Anders, "so there can be no possibility of misunderstanding. Torrie, please bring me my pen and ink—you'll find paper in the top bureau drawer. We'll each sign these articles as a token of good faith, and the man who raises a voice against his appointed duty shall be considered guilty of mutiny against the rest of us."

Almost frantically they agreed. While they clustered around him, Thomas sat down with a board across his lap; his pen spread a rapid flow of words across the page. It didn't take long. The best shots among them were appointed to regular hunt duty, to fetch food for the whole train—there would be no hoarding. The other men were divided into groups, some to scout ahead, some to tend herd, some to make camp and break it, whatever their abilities dictated. The women, girls, even the younger children had their chores set forth in the easy curving script that raced from Anders' pen. Finally, he wrote into the articles that the leader should be the arbiter of all disputes and would assume the over-all responsibility of pacing the train at its best speed. When he was done, he signed it. One by one, the others came forward and set their names on the bottom of the page. When it came Jess's turn, he took up the pen and made an "X" with two hard black strokes, then strode off and started yoking the oxen.

By noon they were on the move, nineteen wagons in all. A light rain was coming down—it smelled of autumn.

That caravan was one that Torrie was to remember in the years afterward in a few vivid pictures, the rest of it—a blur. The land they passed through was uneven and difficult. Jess, for his part of their common effort, now had to spend much of his time helping the other drivers, many of whom were inept with their teams as well as weary and afraid. In order for the train to make its best time, he and a few other men who knew the ways of oxen ranged constantly up and down the long line of wagons, putting their efforts to use wherever the going was roughest, hitching and unhitching teams with twice the expeditiousness of the less adept drivers.

Since Jess couldn't be with their own wagon all the time, Liza took to sitting up in the front seat, even walking some of the way, with the whip ready to keep the animals moving. As for Thomas, he was always away now, doing double work as a huntsman and scout, inspecting the terrain ahead, deciding which slight deviation in the trail would be easiest to cross and how far the train should go each day.

Torrie's main share of the assigned work came after camp was made, but on the very first day she had discovered a new place where she was needed.

They had just come into a particularly bumpy stretch when she thought to go back to the rear of the wagon to see how Cal was taking it. When they had started he'd told them bluffly that he felt pretty good, he'd make out all right. They had cushioned the broken leg as well as possible and then, of necessity, turned to the chores of getting under way. Since then, there hadn't been a sound from him. It was just an offhand thought that sent Torrie back to make sure the boy was comfortable.

At first glance, she saw that he was having a hard time. His short-cropped sandy hair was wet with perspiration, and his hands were clamped on the side of the wagon to brace himself. Just then they hit a bad chuckhole and he stiffened in pain, though he tried not to let Torrie see it.

Laying a hand on his forehead, she was shocked at his feverish warmth.

"Don't say anything!" he warned her harshly between clenched teeth. "Don't tell 'em. Just say I'm all—" Another jarring lurch of the wagon made him catch his breath and chew down hard on his lip.

"Wait—wait a minute—let me—" Hastily, urgently, Torrie sank on her knees, put an arm around him. "No, that won't help. Wait—" She sat down and eased his shoulders into her lap and, when the next jolt came, she managed to save him some of the shock of it. Searching for a comfortable position where she could protect him from the sidewise sway of the hard-bedded old vehicle, she finally found a good grip. Little by little, the wiry young body began to relax against her and Cal closed his eyes.

They rode that way, hour after hour, and in those next days, Torrie came to wonder how she could have felt so full of disdain for Cal only a few months ago. The grit

155

with which he took this punishment filled her with respect. He seemed puzzled by her constant care and looked at her sometimes with the question written plain on his open boyish face. It made her ashamed of all the times she'd badgered him. What had it all been for, the little meanness?

Of one thing she was sure. It wasn't Cal who had changed. He was still the fervent positive hard-eyed little brother, even though his boniness was filling out with solid flesh. Neither had Father changed. Or Mother. The difference was all due to some transformation in herself—now Torrie was sure of it. And it even occurred to her that the reason she had hated them all in those days was that she had really hated herself and was trying to visit the rest of them with her own misery. She'd hated herself for not being grown, and kept herself a child by her very discontent.

But if she didn't feel like a child any more, she still couldn't claim to feel very old or wise. In learning to understand a few things, she was coming to realize more deeply how complex some problems could be. Particularly, she was disturbed over Jess.

Whatever was tormenting him, he'd been keeping away from all of them ever since the night of the birthday party. Just as at first, he was taking his meals to one side, and answered them only in short "Yes'ms" and "No, sirs." She kept remembering the way he'd made that crude mark on the articles—the signature of an illiterate—almost as if he were determined to seem ignorant.

She'd asked Father afterward whether Jess couldn't write his name by now.

"Of course he can!" Thomas said, and he too looked perplexed, although there was no time in those days to contemplate personal questions very long.

156

Anders' leadership, his strict impartiality and firm control, was having a miraculous effect on the morale of the rest of the train. When the others saw that his own wagon took its turn at the end of the line, in the course of the daily rotation, and when they realized that no family was getting more or less meat than the rest of them, it stiffened their spirits and made them bend wholeheartedly into the tasks of the road. By the time they reached the Soda Springs, they looked liked a different lot, and oddly enough a better friendship for one another had come to life as their fears lessened. Cheerfully they badgered Thomas to let the train rest a day at the watering spot.

They had reached it about noon, a welcome sight after the long miles of desolate country. The Springs bubbled in a verdant little valley—Thomas looked at it as longingly as the rest of them. The signs of care were plainer in his face, the lines creased deeper around his eyes, now that the group responsibility was his.

Shaking his head reluctantly, he said, "One day's time may mean the difference between life and death in a snowstorm a month or so from now. We must push on tomorrow morning."

They didn't argue with him. But, for one truant afternoon, chores were happily forgotten by common consent. The men went downstream and the girls went upstream. They swam and washed their hair, rinsed out their clothes as they sat around gossiping in the cool sunshine.

The girls weren't so toplofty as in those first days on the trail. Nor did they treat Torrie like a child any more. Having washed dishes elbow to elbow for two weeks, they had all come to tolerate each other with the false sweetness of marriageable young women. They chattered about men—it had the same flavor that Torrie remembered from long ago, at home, where the silly schoolgirls had laid plots to "get" boys and how to lure them into marriage. While they talked, Torrie sat silent, wondering almost angrily why it should be necessary to have all these tricks and plans. She couldn't help thinking that all this was made to order for the conceit of men like Luke Egan. With a plain honest man, why shouldn't straight simple talk be enough?

She looked out across the open fields where the stock grazed. As she made braids in her long hair, which was almost dry after its washing, she was watching for a familiar figure to come up from the swimming hole below. For the hundredth time, she questioned herself silently. Could it have been the change in her looks that day, some new awareness of her that had set Jess off into this mood?

On an impulse she wound the braids around her head and pinned them there, then bent over to look at herself in a pool of quiet water. The grave dark eyes looked back at her out of a face that was womanly and tremulous—or was it that the water trembled and blurred the image?

When she saw Jess coming, she got up and went across the grass to meet him. Some wind, high above, was driving the clouds furiously, racing overhead. Just as Jess looked up and saw her, one of the bright shafts of sunlight fell upon him and was quickly followed by a cloud shadow. For a minute he seemed about to turn aside, then changed his mind and came doggedly on toward her.

In one hand, he carried a small bundle of washing. He was wearing his coarse Osnaburg shirt and a pair of borrowed denim breeches that were too short for his long legs. As if aware of the shabbiness of his appearance, he stopped in front of her in an attitude of deliberate servility.

"Yes'm?" he said, with a trace of the old resentful mockery.

"I wanted to talk with you, Jess," Torrie said, quaking inwardly but trying to make the words come out straight and unafraid. "There's something wrong—I feel that it's my fault, but I don't know why or what I've done."

"You've done nothing," he said in a low voice, and his look moved restlessly away from hers, glancing around. They stood exposed to everyone's sight here in the midst of the field. "Where do you want to go?" he said.

"I don't want to go anywhere," she told him naïvely.

"It's not a good idea," he insisted, "for us to linger out here. People might think I was stepping out of my place, keeping company with a young lady."

"What do you mean by 'your place'?" she asked earnestly. "Jess, you spoke of that before, when you broke away from us down at Fort Bridger. Yes, you did break away! You don't take your meals with us any more—Cal's been asking why you don't come and look at his leg, and Mother wonders if you're angry about something—"

"Stop it, Torrie." Jess spoke in a hushed sort of torment. "Come on—" He made an urgent little gesture toward the wagon, and this time she let him lead the way toward it. Finally he said, "You're making it almighty hard for me."

"I don't care," she insisted. "I've got to know how you figure things. Because if California is going to be a place where Virginia farmers have to act forever like poor underprivileged people and teachers' daughters have to be haughty and get bowed low to, then I wish we hadn't come!"

Putting it that way, she thought she saw a little uncertainty ease the stern set of his face.

"Don't you understand?" he burst out at last. "There's too far a distance between us." They'd come to where his mare was staked out to graze. Pausing, he ran a hand along her flank. "Maybe she looks some ribby, but she's got good lines where they count. Her back's straight, her legs are good, and she's got a good head—look at this knot between her ears. She's smart. She came from a great pair of racers." He looked down at Torrie now. "There's no substitute for good breeding, Torrie, and that's what I don't have."

As he spoke, a sureness came over Torrie that was almost like a faith. "How do you know?" she demanded. "Maybe if your parents had had schooling, they'd be teachers and I'd be a farm girl. Only I wouldn't be naturally quick like you are. All the handwriting in the world wasn't enough to make me bright, not when it came to being almost hurt by Luke Egan. You knew—everybody else knew—I was being foolish. It's worse being stupid than untaught. And you can't say I didn't come from good parents! It just proves how wrong you are, and if anybody's not fit to be associated with, it's me, not you!" Her voice was rising with agitation. "You must think poorly of a girl who's let herself get kissed by a loud-mouth rough? And I don't blame you!" Turning, she walked away as fast as she could without breaking into a run.

Jess didn't follow. When Torrie reached the wagon and climbed in, one swift glance showed her that he was still standing out in the pasture, absently stroking the mare.

SEPTEMBER

IT WAS growing more and more evident that their food wasn't going to last. The few supplies they had been able to buy at Fort Bridger were almost gone, and ever since the train had left the Snake River, cutting south across the dry wasteland where even the sage was stunted, there had been no game to speak of. A flight of geese had come over early one morning and the men had brought down six of them. Other than that, they'd been spending their ammunition on jack rabbits, which were meager fare, considering the number of people sharing them. Some of the emigrants still had a little dried meat left, but most had only flour and corn-meal, lard hoarded up and doled out by the spoonful. It was plain that they'd have to start butchering the extra stock soon, but these were so lean that their meat wouldn't last the company long.

They were all beginning to wonder where, out in all that empty land ahead, the Humboldt River might be. Since they'd left the Snake, the little streams they were able to find were sometimes two days apart. They carried what water they could, but the stock, wearied from the long journey, couldn't haul much more weight.

And then there came a day when even on the second evening there was no watering place. Thomas and the other men had scouted ahead as broadly as they dared, but had found only a drying mud bottom, token of a waterhole already exhausted by earlier trains.

That next morning, the cattle were bawling with thirst. The children had begun to stare at the elders with mute questioning. Dry lips and parched throats could not even take a meager breakfast of fried mush. The milk from the few cows—all of them almost dry now—had to be given to the sick. Liza gave theirs to Mrs. Peggs, whose baby was failing, little by little.

As they gathered miserably before the campfire, Thomas spoke to them, his own voice husky and raw. "I propose to slaughter one of my oxen this morning. The marrow will go to the children, the inner parts to the feeblest among us. The rest of it we will divide as equally as possible." Then, with faint distaste, he added, "It is well known among the mountain men that raw meat is more nutritive than cooked meat. I might add that there is also more moisture in it. However, it is your affair how you choose to use your own portion." Beckoning to the men, he went to get the tired beast—one which he had bought in Independence—and they led it away toward a secluded spot.

The women stood around silent. Some of them were frowning with repugnance at the thought of uncooked flesh, but many of them were coming to wear an expression of tired patience and determination to do what was necessary to stay alive and get on, as quickly as possible. When the men came back with the meat an hour later, each one took a portion. Wordlessly they dispersed to their own wagons.

Out under the crisp September sunlight behind the Anders wagon, Thomas set forth their own share on the cutting board. Without wasting time, he sliced a thin strip and ate it while the others watched. Nodding to them, he said, "This will do very well."

Cal, propped up in the back opening of the wagon, said stanchly between cracked lips, "I'll try some that way."

Father sliced him a strip. Liza accepted a portion. Torrie hesitated. She felt Jess watching her, almost as if this were some test.

"I'll have a little." She nodded coolly. And when Father handed her a strip, she set about eating it as if it were the most commonplace thing in the world—to chew on raw beef. It was still unpleasantly warm, and the stringy toughness almost made her stomach turn over, but the juices did ease the dryness of her throat and she almost forgot the taste in the satisfaction of seeing Jess visibly trying to brace himself to attack his own share.

Now let him call me a fine lady, she thought with relish.

With what energies they had left, they went on westward all that day, and in midafternoon sighted a far-off straggle of trees breaking the gray roll of the land. Scenting water now, the cattle needed no urging to lurch ahead as fast as they could drag the heavy wagons, and, an hour later, the whole company was splashing in the fresh clear water. With a touch of hysteria, they threw it on each other and some of the men plunged into it headfirst, as silly as children. Torrie felt the same overwrought relief—she almost forgot Cal in her own rush to drink at the river, but after the first grateful swallow, she remembered him and went a little sheepishly to get the dipper, only to discover that Father had already carried the boy down and set him on the bank where he could reach the water himself.

"The Humboldt!" shouted Mr. Peggs, dancing a little jig, funny as only a fat man can be. "From here on, it's fresh water all the way! We're practically on the golden sunny shores right now, friends!"

Thomas Anders smiled with the rest of them, but Torrie saw him look toward the mountains stretching away to the south. She had been watching them too, as they loomed higher on the horizon each day. Fierce heights, reaching upward in jagged impenetrability. They were near enough now to see patches of clean white in the crevasses. Torrie turned to her father, dismayed.

"Is that fresh snow!"

"I'd say so." And then he glanced around at the empty plains. "Do you realize that we've not seen another train since we left Fort Hall?" he murmured thoughtfully. There had been a few Oregon-bound trains along the Snake. "I had supposed that when we reached the Humboldt we'd be in company again with other migrators to California."

"The Donners! They should have been here by now."

He nodded anxiously.

"Up there in the Sierras?" She looked at the mountains with a shiver.

"No, Victoria," he said gently. "The Sierras are somewhere out to the west, far ahead."

That night they took close inventory of their food and extra stock. Even counting the possibility of butchering the milk cows, there wasn't enough to last them more than another few weeks.

No one knew exactly how far it was to the Sierras, but when they pooled the various reports they'd heard, they were agreed on one fact: it was said to take a wagon train the better part of a month to cross the Nevada country, and at the end of the long drag was the worst mountain crossing of the whole trail.

"They say," Mr. Beckwith offered tentatively, "that when some of the folks last year ran low on food, they sent ahead to Sutter's post for supplies."

Thomas nodded. "I've been thinking of Mr. Sutter, myself. He is supposedly a helpful friend to the emigration. But I'm afraid by the time we cross the state, there will be no time for a relief party to go to the Fort and return to us. If we wait much longer to send ahead, it will be too late."

"Well now"—Beckwith retreated quickly—"I didn't say we ought to send out right away. There's a lot of territory out there that's not safe to be crossed by just two or three men alone. They say the Injuns out yonder are the vilest in the country."

"What Indians?" Father demanded. "I didn't know we were coming into hostile lands. We're out of Shoshoni country now and too far north for the Apache—"

"These are what they call 'Diggers,'" Beckwith told him, and several of the other men nodded. "They're castoffs from the other tribes, low-minded scum that don't even know how or care enough to hunt, but live by scavenging and grubbing roots."

"And rifling wagon trains," added Peggs, round-eyed. "I heard that last year and year before, the emygrators had to shoot a good many of 'em on account of their thievery, and ever since, the Diggers has had it in for the whites, claw and tommyhawk. It's a risky business crossing that stretch alone."

One of the other men spoke up. "That ain't no part of what we signed up for."

Father stifled a small sigh. "No, it's no man's bounden duty, but we may live or die in so far as someone will volunteer. Inasmuch as I'm leader of the train, I will offer my services for this job."

"Not you, Tom!" Beckwith shook his head. "We need you here."

And the others chorused their protests so quickly that Father spread his hands out to quiet them. "I'll serve in whatever capacity you wish, but I think you'd better reconsider. If this trip takes a wagon train a month, a man on horseback should be able to make it in ten days and back in even less, as the train moves forward to meet him. . . ."

"No, not you," they repeated again. And then there was a silence around the campfire, women staring anxiously at their husbands—you could see them get set to protest if their men were to be sent on such a mission.

"I'll go." It was Jess who spoke, standing up abruptly, lanky and hard-eyed in the guttering light of the fire. The others turned in surprise, for he seldom said a word at these meetings. "It's right and fit that I should," he added, as if the matter were settled. "I've got no wife or young'uns to watch out for, and I've got two good horses."

It seemed to relieve their minds overwhelmingly. All seemed happy to accept his offer except Thomas. Amid the murmurs of approval, he admonished them curtly. "Gentlemen! This is just a boy! You'd surely not allow him to make such a dangerous journey alone. I won't hear of it. There'll have to be at least one other volunteer."

That silenced them again, and no man seemed to want to look his neighbor in the eye.

With a trace of a smile, Jess spoke across the fire to Thomas. "I'll either go alone or I won't go."

Torrie, like all the others, had been shocked by the suddenness of it all, but now she felt a hurtful twisting inside, almost as bad as that she'd felt, a minute ago, when Father had volunteered. She could hardly believe her eyes when she saw Thomas nod quietly at Jess.

"I understand. I'll say no more against it. You must do as you think best."

The strange wording of that reply didn't occur to Torrie until later. There was such a bustle, getting together what little Jess was to take; blankets, ammunition for the Colt revolver, which Father insisted he carry for protection. And, for the horses, the last of the little precious grain that had been hidden away for the stock in case of dire emergency.

"I insist you take it," Father said firmly. "The swift accomplishment of your purpose may well depend on the well-being of your mounts. The hopes of all of us are riding with you." And that was that.

Few of the other outfits came through with any contribution, although one or two offered remnants of food and all were full of advice. However, not one would put up any money—they wouldn't even admit they had any. So in the end Liza sat up half the night unstitching part of the quilt to give Jess their own banknotes for payment to Sutter for the supplies they would need.

That next morning, the Virginian was silent as he went about putting a pack on the buckskin, although the other emigrants who had gathered around were making twice as much noise as usual, as if to cover some common embarrassment.

Torrie, who had lain awake most of the night trying to untangle her own emotions, was weary and distressed as she went to and from the wagon helping Mother bring some last-minute necessities—a small sack of sugar, a bottle of brandy that Torrie hadn't even known they had. Afterward, she hardly remembered what she had done to help.

All she could think of was that Jess would be riding out alone with his own private bitter thoughts, across that endless sagebrush wasteland. Anxiously she racked her brain for something to send with him, to dispel that terrible loneliness—and all she could think of was a book. He'd got such relief from the speller—but she couldn't give him one of Father's, and the only one that was really hers was an advanced reader from the seventh grade, which seemed a poor gift. And yet—she dug down under the mattress to where her trunk was, found the well-thumbed little volume, and rushed back out where they all stood, giving Jess last-minute encouragement.

Finally Father dispersed them, kindly but positively, saying, "Jess is as ready as he'll ever be. I believe the rest of us had better get to the business of breaking camp." And when they had scattered back to their own wagons, he turned to the Virginian, troubled. "Jess," he said quietly, "you don't owe us this. I want you to understand that what you're doing is a benefaction to us all—no part of the duties you hired on for."

"I hired on to get to California," Jess said. "Looks like I'm going to see it sooner than I figured."

Liza burst out abruptly. "I've got to say how I'm grateful for the way you fixed Cal's leg. It's doing so fine—" Only

168

it was easy to tell that she meant much more that she couldn't put in words.

"I'm glad." The Virginian nodded his head slightly. He was getting ready to mount when Torrie spoke up.

"Could I walk along with you down to the trees there?" It came in a burst and sounded terribly forward; she flushed painfully as they all looked at her.

Slowly, a little awkwardly, Jess said, "I'd be pleased."

Side by side, without talking, they went down through the camp and out of the wagon corral, Jess leading the two horses and Torrie clutching the book half-hidden in her skirts.

When they were well out of earshot of the others, she said, "I guess you think this is just more of my boldness, asking to walk with you, but I don't care. You've already thought a lot of things about me that can't be changed."

Oddly, Jess laughed, looking out across the land ahead as if searching for something. And Torrie wondered how she could have supposed him to be hard-faced last night; this morning the deep-set young eyes were troubled and shy.

He said, "There's nothing I've thought about you yet that *hasn't* somehow been changed. First I couldn't help thinking you were a little girl, I treated you short and disrespectful, even. Then, all of a sudden, there you were with your hair all soft and tucked up and that green dress on—" He shook his head at the memory. "You looked a way out of my reach. I had to start thinking a new way about you, and then—" He hesitated. "Then you said this was a fresh country where a woman and a man should be judged for whatever they are and not where they come from. That's a stumper. I don't know about me—whatever

I'm good for, I haven't found out yet."

"But you do know! You know where you're going and what you want—"

"Haven't tried it, though. Talk comes easy. I haven't proved a thing, have I?"

"Is that why you're going on this risky business—to prove yourself?"

"I'm going because somebody's got to," he told her flatly, "or none of us is like to get there. Just between you'n me, I'm scared."

They had reached the clump of trees, and once out of sight of the camp Jess turned to face her. "But what I wanted to say is that since you gave me what-for that day at the Soda Springs—oh yes, you did—since then I had to think of you different all over again." He shook his head, as if faced with some difficult problem.

"How?" she asked wonderingly.

Jess took a deep breath. "Well, I'll tell you this—what you were worried about, that a man would think bad of you for being kissed by a big rough randy fellow who forced himself on you, which wasn't really your fault— much— Well, what I wanted to say is, it's too bad you had that trouble with Luke, but it doesn't make any difference to—anybody—at least, except you, and you mustn't get the feeling that all men are—I mean, don't think that it isn't a perfectly right and true thing for a man to—under the right conditions—" He bogged down hopelessly at that point. Turning, red-faced, with a leap he got himself up across the mare's back and swung astraddle.

"Wait!" Torrie remembered the book and held it out to him. "I wanted you to have something. This isn't much, but—"

170

Silently he took the little volume, turned one or two of its pages with a cautious finger, and then looked down at her. "You mean this is mine? You're giving me this?"

"Well, yes. Of course, it isn't new, but—"

Carefully, Jess put it into the saddlebag on the buckskin and turned back to her. "Just because you've read it, too, you think that makes it worth *less?* You put a curious value on some things. You even got riled when I called you a lady. I meant no insult by it. What I call a lady is somebody who'll swallow down raw meat when there's a need to and look handsome doing it, and if you don't understand what I mean, maybe I'll have it figured out how to tell you when I see you again."

Wheeling the mare, he took off across the sage flats at a long lope, the buckskin lining out behind. Torrie waited, watching him go with a pounding inside her that almost made her dizzy. She waited until he was only an outline in the morning twilight that still hung heavy over the western prairie. And once, from far off out there, she thought he looked back and waved.

A wind blew in their faces all that day, and toward afternoon it began to carry in from the northwest a scud of lead-colored clouds. It caused an eerie effect—the sun still out all around them, sharp-lighting the near lands, and beyond it the heavy shadow of the storm. A flight of little birds were blown across the somber face of the sky—for an instant they glinted with sunlight like bits of silver paper, and then were gone.

As early darkness settled in, they drove the wagons into the nightly circle. By now the air was shiveringly cold,

171

and it was a relief for the emigrants to finish off their scant supper and scurry to their beds.

Huddled down under the comforters, Torrie thought of Jess. He hadn't been dressed very heavily—just the coat of homespun over his shirt, and the homespun breeches, all patches by now. He had carried an extra woolen coat of Father's that Liza had urged upon him at the last minute, and in his bedroll was one of their warmest blankets, but what good would any of that do against the inward chill of danger?

Torrie pictured him, crouched beside some small flickering spot of fire, a prick of light lost in the immense dark spaces, trying to warm away the cold knowledge of isolation. He must be listening . . . but not for the little animal noises. It was a sudden silence, they said, that usually meant a dangerous presence. And how do you listen for a nothingness?

She fell asleep uneasily on the drift of her thoughts while the wind racked the old wagon and shivered its canvas top. It seemed only a minute later that she wakened with a start, nudged by an insistent finger—Cal poking her in the ribs.

"Torrie!" he whispered fearfully. "Listen . . . !"

"What is it?" She came alert, her heart pumping hard. The wind had died and everything was still except for the soft sound that she couldn't place—so gentle, it was more sensed than heard, like a woman's fingers feeling across the canvas top above them, groping for something.

Torrie struggled to sit up, and then, out of the darkness at the far end of the wagon, Father spoke quietly.

"Don't be alarmed, children. There's no immediate danger, but—it *is* snowing."

172

OCTOBER

"WHAT DO you mean! The river—the *Humboldt River* —drops out of sight! It's just gone?" Mr. Beckwith demanded with the same dismay that the rest of them were feeling.

Thomas, who had ridden back to tell them, nodded wearily. "I wondered why the trail was veering away from it so sharply," he said. "We'd better fill our water containers."

But it was hard to take. The river had been the only source of comfort across those endless miles of Nevada. Even though game had been getting scarcer every day, the boon of water had helped sustain them through many meager meals. To have to leave it now was almost more than they could bear.

Mrs. Peggs burst into tears. "I don't believe it! My husband said we'd have water all the way to California!"

Thomas answered her with that patience that never left him. "I'd hoped he was right, too, but I'd heard that the Humboldt sinks into the earth, and that's apparently the

exact truth. A mile or so from here it widens into a dangerous flat swampy area. The ground seems to be porous, allow-
ing the water to seep into underground recesses. I couldn't
venture into it even a few hundred yards on horseback.
Wagons would bog down at once. We'll simply have to
take a safe distance around it and hope—pray—that the
stretch between here and the next river is not too lengthy.
Remember, others have made it."

So they went about doing as he'd told them, but their
endurance was near the cracking point. It had been a hard
month. Even though the weather had cleared after that first
flurry of snow, and the going along the river had been
roughly passable, it had taken a lot of effort when they had
little left to spend. Every man, woman, and child of the
train was acutely conscious of the crisping days, the early
setting of the sun; and the shortness of food was like a
specter riding at their shoulders. Even the Sierras, which
had come into view as a crooked blue outline on the western
horizon, afforded the travelers little encouragement. True,
they were near their destination now, but there was something terrible about that barrier stretching away to north
and south that put a new desperation in them.

This took itself out in many ways, surliness toward each
other, foolish accusations; erstwhile friendships vanished,
and there were fights up and down the train. The strain
of sharing the dwindling food would have driven them
apart in twenty different directions had it not been for
Father's stern control. He had a way of shaming the worst
complainants in his quiet courteous manner, and so far had
kept them sullenly striving together. But now, without the
one blessing of water, their resentments were flying thick
and fast.

They needed some target, and the focus of their frustration was gradually coming to bear on the Peggs family. They hadn't had any extra stock to contribute to the common table, and Mrs. Peggs was too weak to do much of the work of cooking and washing. Mr. Peggs was no good at all with a rifle; although pitifully willing to try, his efforts were just a waste of ammunition, and he wasn't much better on a horse, or driving oxen. The pudgy little fellow —not so plump now as in earlier days—tried to make up for his ineptness. Apologetically he worked over the simpler chores of gathering brush for the fires and standing guard over the herd, but some members of the train, prodded by a big coarse-faced farmer named Scott, began to blame him for being "bad luck."

"Foolish superstitious talk," Thomas labeled it angrily, but the grumbling was growing, especially since the Anders' milk cow couldn't be slaughtered so long as it gave the few cups of milk that were keeping the Peggs baby alive.

Now as they headed out over the dry land, there were open proposals to banish the poor fuddled family from the train. Scott said it as callously as if it wouldn't mean almost certain death to all three of them.

"He was so cock-and-bull about the Humboldt goin' clean to California!" the burly red-faced man growled. "Remember that? He's a Jonah, that's what. Him and his talk about these-here Diggers that never showed up."

That was another thing that was irritating the men— the need to stand sentry duty each night. Although they broke the hours up into watches, it meant that all of them had to put in long heavy-eyed stints riding around the camp, peering out into the darkness, on the lookout for Indians that had not yet materialized.

That night, it was necessary for Thomas to speak to them sharply. "Hasn't it occurred to you that perhaps the reason we've not been subject to marauders is that this guard has been posted? In this venture," he added grimly, "there is no time for these mean maunderings. It wastes the energies and dries the throat. We will keep watch tonight as always. I'll take the first stand."

"And I'll take the morning watch," spoke up Peggs, eager to ingratiate himself.

"No, Henry, you stood guard only last night—" Father began to object, but Peggs looked so painfully anxious that at last he shrugged. "Very well, but I don't like it. It's not proper for a man to do more than his share of night duty."

"And what about you, sir?" Peggs said timidly. "You've done double shares of all our work. You shouldn't take night watch at all."

Father brushed his protest aside with a small despairing gesture. "What difference which of us worked hardest if all of us perish?"

They gathered around the campfire, a hostile silent crew, and dipped into the pot of stew which the women had made—a thin mixture brewed from the remnants of the skin and hoofs of the last spare ox. They'd boiled up, with it, a few handfuls of dried beans—that was all.

Cal ate his fairly well, but Torrie almost gagged at the first taste. Thinking of Jess's last words to her, she tried to down a little of it with an outward show of fortitude, but when they had all finished she'd hardly eaten enough to keep her stomach from sticking together.

Helping Caleb back to the wagon—he was able to hobble now on makeshift crutches—Torrie said, "I guess Jess would change his mind about me after tonight. He thought

I was so brave to eat the raw beef that day."

A couple of months ago, that would have drawn a smart retort from Cal. Now, he just said soberly, "I miss Jess." And then he added, "You know what they're all saying? Scott and the others?"

"How do you know what they're saying?" she asked.

"I heard 'em. Scott and somebody else were riding along-side the wagon yesterday and they said Jess wasn't coming back, because why should he? It's dangerous to come back and what would he gain by it? They said they knew it all along—he's got our money now so he'll keep on going."

Torrie laughed shortly. "They don't know Jess very well."

"Of course not," Cal said matter-of-factly. "I know he wouldn't do that. But they're saying he should have been back by now, and it has been nearly four weeks, which should have been long enough, you'd think. So I was won-dering if maybe he got scalped or et by a bear."

"Eaten!" Torrie corrected him sharply. "And don't say such a terrible thing! It's too awful even to think of."

Cal looked up at her. "You like Jess a lot, don't you?"

"He's—" Torrie hesitated, but she couldn't really tell anybody just how she felt about Jess. "He's the most stub-born man I ever met," she said.

"Well, you're stubborn too," Cal commented frankly, "so I guess that's why he likes you."

"He does? What makes you think so?" she demanded, passing over the appraisal of herself.

Cal grinned. "Well, I'll tell you a secret, only I'm not supposed to. You know why he let me ride the buckskin all that time? Because I showed him how to spell your name." Then, thoughtfully, he added, "I guess that's the best bargain I ever made."

Torrie was so hungry that she couldn't sleep well that night but swam up out of the shallows of drowsiness at the least sound. She heard Father come to bed, sometime in the early hours, and a little later she heard the coyotes start their long chain of howling, from ridge to ridge. She drifted off again, and then abruptly she wakened to dead silence.

She lay there, wide-eyed in the darkness. There was something unnatural about this stillness. She heard her father stir and rise on one elbow. . . .

And then the air was split by an agonizing bellow. It brought all of them bolt upright in bed. Thomas snatched the rifle and lunged over the tailgate out into the darkness.

"He didn't even put his boots on!" Liza moaned.

Cal crawled up front to see what was happening, for now the night was full of the wild bawling of the cattle and the shouts of men running. Someone cried shrilly. "There they go, get 'em, the stinkin' red buzzards, shoot 'em!"

And another voice was yelling, "The cattle—look out, they're headin' your way!"

In a rush of hoofs, the herd stampeded past, down to the far end of the wagon corral.

Torrie and Liza were getting into their clothes as fast as they could.

At last it seemed to be over and the noise outside settled down into harsh tones of disgust. "How many did we lose?" somebody demanded.

"Looks like seven or eight head. Look at that, call that an arrow? I could make better arrows when I was a kid. These are no-account scrub Injuns for sure."

"This cow's been knifed in the belly. It's done for."

"That critter there's been bashed with a club, looks like."
Father's voice came through the chaos. "Gentlemen.
We'll need some more lanterns, and you'd better dress
against this cold wind—"

Mother was already lighting their own lamp now that
the danger was past. Thomas appeared briefly in the back
opening to take it from her.

"Diggers," he told them briefly. "You'd best stay inside,
all of you. This is not a pretty sight. Some of the wounded
cattle aren't quite dead—"

Torrie shuddered.

"Here, put on your boots and coat—" Liza pressed them
upon him. Then she said, "Where was Mr. Peggs? Why
didn't he give warning?"

"Apparently," Father said, as he dressed, "the poor fellow couldn't stay awake—went sound asleep slumped over
in the saddle. I've sent him to his wagon and told him to
stay there for his own safety. The mood of the men is somewhat unsteady. Torrie, please get out the paper we signed
—I may need it. Thank you. And just in case it should be
necessary—" He set the rifle inside the tailgate where it
would be handy. Then he left them, to wonder soberly
what his preparations might mean.

When he'd gone, Liza lit the other lantern and the three
of them sat silent, listening. . . .

"By Jerry, Tom Anders," somebody roared, "I'm not
gonna be turned aside!"

Cal, from his post up front, whispered excitedly, "That's
old Scott. He wants to hang Mr. Peggs."

"Oh dear Lord!" Liza closed her eyes as if she were
praying.

"We're gonna set up my wagon tongue," Scott yelled,

"and right here'n now, we're gonna cast out the devil, like the Bible says."

"The Bible says: Thou shalt not kill!" thundered Father. "You'll not harm a member of this train while I live."

Torrie had crowded up beside Cal in the front opening now, she could see Father standing in the midst of them, the articles in his hand, the bobbing lantern light throwing a golden glare over his face. He was the smallest man of that whole tense circle, but something inside him seemed to hold him taller and stronger than all of them. His very rage, rare as it was, seemed to subdue them.

"What are your signatures worth?" He shook the articles at them. "Are your names worth the paper they're written on? Then you will cease at once to agitate yourselves for the punishment of a poor innocent."

"I dunno what you're protectin' that fat fool for," Scott snarled. "Three of them dead critters is yours."

Thomas didn't flicker an eyelash. "My oxen are no more important than yours, and no less. We've suffered a loss; we will not return the animals to life by debate or blame-seeking. If you care to carp, direct your irritation at me— I allowed Mr. Peggs to stand a watch I didn't approve. Any man who is worn out from too many nights awake can be overwhelmed by sleep. If you want my opinion, this fruit-less bicker is likely to cost us dearly unless we stop it and get to work. The animals that have been killed must be butchered quickly. I advise you to assess your losses, take as much meat as you can carry—lighten your wagons of other cargo if necessary. Do not sacrifice either food or water in favor of valuables you may never live to use. By sunup, we must be on the trail again."

Under the positive authority of his tone, the men seemed

180

to get their bearings. Together they walked to where the dead and dying cattle lay sprawled on the ground and began the stark business of finishing the beasts off. Torrie turned away sickly.

Liza was watching her with open anxiety. "You're not looking too good, I noticed you didn't eat much last night."

Cal also turned back now and remarked, "Torrie was smart. I ate some of that stuff and I threw it up." With a fiendish humor, he turned to Torrie. "How would you like to have a big slice of hot baked ham with creamed peas and sweet potatoes?"

"I'll break your other leg if you go on," Torrie groaned.

Liza had gone over to rummage under the bedclothes. When she turned, there was a tenderness in her face that made it look years younger. "Now that we have fresh meat again, I guess I'm taking no chance to give you this. I kept thinking you might need something later, but I'm not sure this isn't the time to shore up your strength right now." She set forth on a napkin a small assortment of scraps—odds and ends of corncakes and dried meat, part of a shriveled onion and a couple of small fish that Torrie recognized as the last of a catch they had salted down, away back when they first started along the Humboldt.

"Fish'll make you thirst some," Liza added, "but I reckon we can allow a little water."

"But where—?" Torrie began incoherently. And then she guessed. "This is *your* food! Mother, you haven't been eating all your share!"

Liza said carelessly, "Oh, I don't need much. Young folks take more to keep 'em filled. Go on and eat it."

They didn't argue—they just couldn't. Both of them dug

181

in and attacked the old victuals as if they were a rare delicacy while Liza looked on with a smile.

Torrie was glad that she didn't have to go through that next morning on an empty stomach. It was hard enough on her innards to watch the beautiful old mahogany bureau get hoisted down out of the wagon with all their silver in it, Father's writing materials, their extra clothes. All that they were going to keep was the boxes of books—Father had put it up to a vote and no one in the family had spoken a word against those, knowing what a tremendous store he put by them.

"The foundations for so many things," Thomas had said wistfully. "Yes, I believe we should try to take them."

But now as Cal watched them unload his belongings, the saddle and the buffalo skull and the precious box of rocks that he'd been collecting, he had a hard time sounding nonchalant as he said, "I just wish we could take a couple of those rocks along. There's probably gold in 'em."

Father considered the matter gravely. "Do you think so?" And he took time to study the rocks a minute.

"See—right there. Isn't that gold?"

"No, son, I'm sorry to say those are pyrites; gold ore seldom if ever shows such brilliance. Possibly you'll find better pickings in California—at least, we must keep an eye open when we get there."

Meanwhile Liza and Torrie were hurrying to cut the meat into strips that would dry, rushing their work because the other wagons were yoking up now and the day was broadening in the east.

Several of the families who had lost oxen had decided

to team together, abandoning one of the wagons and going on in the other, but when Mr. Peggs came over, almost tearfully, and begged the Anders family to share their wagon with them, Liza looked across at her husband imploringly and Thomas understood. To Peggs, he said, "Thank you, but I believe we shall try to bring our own outfit through."

They had trouble putting the Guernsey into the yoke with the extra ox, to make a team. Weak as she was, the scrawny old cow plunged and bawled at such an indignity, but finally they managed to pull out at an uneven gait on the heels of the rest of the train.

Thomas stayed with them to drive the mismatched cattle until they were broken in to each other, but as the sun came up, he said, "I'm afraid I must leave you, my dear. Mr. Peggs has promised to help you with the oxen. I've got to find out what's ahead and when we can expect to reach water."

It never ended, Torrie thought numbly. Go on and on, looking for one more river and then one more.

As Father was getting ready to swing up onto the old black horse, Beckwith came galloping back toward them along the train with Duncan and Scott at his heels.

"Look—look at this!" He was waving a piece of paper in his hand. "Found it on a pile of rock just ahead."

They all looked a little sheepish, and Scott even wore a hollow grin. "If we'd just gone on a mile more last evenin'," he said, "maybe we'd have all been up night-watchin'."

Father took the bit of paper, puzzled, and unfolded it. Torrie leaned to look over his shoulder, and read the words herself, even as he repeated them aloud:

The words were carefully printed, evidently with a burned end of stick. The paper itself was dirty and creased from the rocks that had weighted it down—it looked many weeks old. But he had got this far alive. She let out a wordless breath of thanks.

"I thought that feller of yours couldn't write," marveled Duncan.

"What I wonder," Beckwith added, "is where he came by a piece of paper out here."

Thomas looked around at them. "The thing that strikes me is that Jess came twenty miles back through dangerous country to leave this. He knew what we'd be feeling about now. This was the act of a man of imagination and courage. A good man."

Torrie reached out stealthily and took the note—her father seemed not to notice, nor did the others. As soon as Anders was mounted, they all rode forward to spread the good news and hurry the pace. Twenty miles—with luck they might even make it by nightfall.

But back inside the wagon alone, Torrie was reading and rereading the neat words. Only two of them *slightly* misspelled. And inwardly she blossomed with pride. To herself, she whispered over again her father's words: A good man.

II

The golden days were over and the sky was heavy above the shoulders of the mountains as they started up that long climb into the Sierras. They had found their river—this

Truckee that they were following. It had been right there, where Jess had said it was. But now the gift of water wasn't enough to sustain men or cattle. They went on because they had no choice. Even their grumbling had slacked off now and their faces were blank or, when they saw an ox stumble, tinged with despair.

Anders had put his own wagon at the rear of the line, for the two yoke were hardly able to drag it up the steepening slope of the mountains and it fell behind a little farther each day; it took longer every evening to catch up with the rest, sometimes until after darkness had settled in. Mother was doing the best she could with the cattle—she and Torrie trudged beside the beasts leading them around the rough spots. But the oxen were weakening visibly. Forage was almost nonexistent; to find even a little dry grass meant searching up the ravines for pockets of hay that hadn't been grazed off by the trains ahead of them.

Their own food was nearly gone again, too. And the way was getting steeper every day. The Sierras loomed above them and around them, as they moved in the shadowy depths of a canyon. Only a thin warmth occasionally reached them at midday what few times the sun shone bleakly through the thickening clouds and sharp cold winds blasted down off the heights.

There had been no further trace of Jess, either. And then one morning, as they were about to break camp, a shout went up. A man was riding down the mountain toward them, leading a string of pack mules. As he came on, it was plain to see that it wasn't Jess. This was a heavy-set man; the mules were being driven by two Indians. But it didn't occur to them to doubt that this was their relief party.

Thomas rode to meet them, with Duncan and Beckwith

and the others. And then, even from a distance, Torrie could see the shock of disappointment on their faces. They brought the stranger back to the fire and he gave them some coffee, the first any of them had even so much as smelled since Fort Hall. While the women brewed it, the men questioned the rider. Father was trying to be courteous, trying not to show what a bitter mortification this was, to find that the food on the mules was not theirs.

The man said his name was Stanton and he was on his way with these supplies to succor the Donner party.

"The Donners are behind us!" Anders exclaimed incredulously.

"Yes, sir, they must be." Stanton shook his head. "I left them near a month ago—they hadn't even reached the Humboldt then. We'd been following a will-o'-the-wisp track that Hastings left, all up and down through the Nevada mountains."

"But, man, if they haven't come up with us—!" Thomas stared at him aghast.

"Yes, I'm afraid for them." Stanton nodded. "Even you will have to hurry to get across if this weather sets in. The Donners must be moving very slowly. They took to fighting among themselves—one man killed another and they banished him from the train. Reed, poor fellow, was just trying to defend himself. They must have been mad to banish him. He came on to Sutter's Fort—that's how I learned of it. He said the train was going to pieces. That stretch after we left Bridger nearly finished us."

"The Wasatch." Thomas nodded grimly. "Did you go down the canyon after Hastings?"

"Good Lord, no!" Stanton swallowed some of his coffee wryly. "We tried to make it across the top, but the descent on the far side broke our wagons and then the desert broke our spirits. The oxen stampeded in the salt storms—we lost over half of them. Some people finished the crossing on foot. It took us over six days and then we came out only half-alive—to face the Nevada country." He shook his head. "Hastings' track seemed to wander all over the place."

"But he got through?"

"Yes, just barely. He's not far ahead of you, going down the other side. I passed his train a week ago. They're limping in, impoverished, but he brought them to California." Stanton laughed mirthlessly. "Most of them haven't enough property to trade for one pair of shoes, much less all that acreage that Hastings hoped to sell them. Sutter's going to have to carry the lot of them on credit until they get on their feet again."

"Mr. Sutter's post must be a busy place," Anders ventured hesitantly, "but we can't help wondering whether you might have noticed our young messenger there? Or on the trail? We had hoped he'd be here by now with our own relief supplies."

"Yes," put in Beckwith earnestly. "Fair-haired man riding a sorrel mare, leading a buckskin."

Stanton looked around at them quickly, then stared hard into the fire. Torrie, who was with the other women on the outskirts of that council, felt her breath clench up inside her. Because it was plain that Mr. Stanton had seen *something!*

"Crossing these mountains," he said slowly, "is an extremely dangerous undertaking, even with plenty of extra stock and armed men for companions. Aside from the precipitous steepness which you will reach above here, there are many Diggers through the mountains. Game is maddeningly scarce. My companion, McCutcheon, who made the trip to Sutter's with me, was too weak to return, even though his family is with the Donners. We barely got to the post and that was some weeks ago—"

"What have you seen or heard of our Mr. Jessen, though?" insisted Thomas quietly.

"I was just explaining that your man might have been too wearied by the crossing to come back or—" He paused and spread his hands. "Well, it would be less than sensible of me not to tell you that I saw near the trail, as I came along a few days ago, the remains of two horses and a man. The wolves hadn't left enough to identify the nature of their demise, but it appeared to be the work of Diggers —there were some crude arrows strewn around."

They swallowed this in silence. Then Thomas said, "Many men must have passed along this trail. It could have been someone else."

"Of course." Stanton nodded quickly. "Yes, it could! And I hope for your sakes that it was. The only thing that struck me as somewhat of a coincidence—I said there wasn't much left of any of them, but there was sufficient evidence that I could tell that one of the horses had been a buckskin."

NOVEMBER

TORRIE HAD never seen her mother cry before!

The hardest crisis they had faced yet was the need for Father to go ahead with the main body of the train. He had looked at Liza with the whole terrible indecision written in his face, and she looked right back at him.

"You signed on to be leader," she had said simply.

And he nodded.

It meant he had to leave them, for their own wagon toiled laboriously up the heartbreaking steep pitch of the mountains some way behind the others, while the clouds lowered over the peaks, daily more threatening. But through it all, Liza had borne up firmly. She and Torrie walked the trail beside the teams, not even wondering aloud how far the others might be ahead, around the twisting turns of the canyon. Always at night, Father came back to help them into camp. But the way was getting steeper, the cattle faltering.

And then one afternoon the snow began to fall. Torrie, turning anxiously to Liza, was frightened to see the tears streaming down that plain weather-worn face.

"Mother!" she gasped. "What is it?"

Liza shook her head. "I don't . . . I don't know . . . Jess . . . I didn't want them to send him . . . I understood him, he was . . . a lot like me in some ways . . . I don't know what's the matter. . . ." Blindly she brushed at her eyes with the weary awkward gesture of a child, and then slowly, almost gently, crumpled onto the ground.

As if by common consent, the oxen stopped. With the clank and screech of the wagon suddenly ended, everything was deathly still.

"Cal!" Torrie screamed. "Come out here quick!"

He seemed to take forever. The cold made his leg ache these days, and he spent most of the time under a pile of quilts. Now, peering from the front opening of the wagon, his gray eyes went wide and terrified as he stared at the huddled form of his mother.

"Help me!" Torrie told him swiftly. "We've got to get her into the wagon."

"Where's Father? I don't see the rest . . ." he quavered. For they were, in truth, alone, curtained in on all sides by the heavy whispering fall of moist snow.

Torrie was trying with some new-found strength to lift her mother's inert body. It was a struggle, but, with Cal pulling and Torrie lifting, they managed to get the unconscious woman inside the wagon. Torrie worked feverishly to get Liza stretched out on the mattress, covered her with every comforter they had, for her skin felt deathly cold and she was white as skim milk.

The medicine bag! She rushed to get it out, dug down and found the smelling salts. Holding them where her mother could breathe the acrid fumes, Torrie watched, while everything stood still inside her. Then, remembering how Jess had chafed Cal's wrists to get his blood moving, Torrie rubbed feverishly at her mother's hands, watching the shallow rise and fall of her breathing. If only there were something hot to drink, she thought helplessly. But they didn't dare light the stove while they were moving—a bad sway could jolt the whole fire out into the wagon. And they had to keep moving! They had to get started again, to try to catch up to Father and the others.

"You've got to take care of her," she told Cal. "Let her breathe the salts. I've got to go and try to get the teams started again."

The boy seemed frozen, staring at his mother's lifeless form. "What's the matter with her?" he whispered hoarsely.

"I don't know, but I'd reckon it came from not eating enough. I'll bet she's been saving back again for us. And she was saying something about Jess—" Torrie's voice almost broke on the word. She had been numbed by the news Stanton had brought them the day before; it just couldn't seem possible to her that Jess had been killed up in those fierce heights ahead of them. She had put it away from her and stanchly clung to her inner belief that it was some mistake—he must be alive. But just now, when Mother had begun to cry, the truth of it—that it really was possible— came over Torrie in a sickening wave, and now all her own grief welled up.

Cal looked at her desperately. "Are you gonna cry?" he yelled.

"No!"

"Well, DON'T!" And then he added bluffly, "Jess isn't killed anyhow. He's too smart!" Squaring his shoulders, he said, "I'll go drive the oxen—"

Even though it was bravado, it steadied Torrie. "You can't walk far on that leg," she said firmly. "You tend Mother."

"My leg's as good as ever—" He moved with her toward the front of the wagon, but as they reached the opening he broke off, staring blankly, his face coming undone again. "Look!"

There in the mud, one of the oxen—the brindle, yoked to the Guernsey—was faltering to its knees. Wearily it sank in its tracks, dragging the cow halfway down with it. Struggling weakly, she finally staggered and lay down beside it, heaving. The other pair of oxen gave up their efforts and just stood with heads hanging.

A moment of panic seized Torrie. "They've got to get up! Make them go on!" She picked up the whip.

But Cal caught her arm. "No, don't whip them," he said. "I don't think they *can* get up. They're done for."

It was a moment frozen in time and space—the sagging cattle, the tall trees rising dimly around them, only half-visible through the thick white haze, snow crystals clustering small and perfect on Cal's sandy-colored eyebrows, and everything around them—quiet.

Almost to her own surprise, Torrie felt calm; the panic came under control. There wasn't, and never would be again, that childlike terror of a minute ago.

Taking a deep breath, she said, "The first thing to do is to build a fire, fast."

Cal hesitated. "The wood'll be wet."

"That's all right. If it's smoky, we can't help it. You

gather what you can that's near around, and I'll go on up the sides of the hills."

"You might not find your way back, and there's Diggers and—"

"Caleb, this talk is wasting time," she said, and thought remotely how much like Father it sounded. Climbing down from the wagon, she reached up to him. "Here—I'll help you—"

"Listen, Torrie, we could build a little fire inside in the stove."

"Come on!" She spoke a little more impatiently. "Do as I say. We've got to keep the cattle from freezing—they're our only hope of getting out of here. Besides, a fire will help Father find us. Now hurry!"

Stiffly he limped off; although his leg was mended nicely now, he hadn't used it much. As she climbed the steep side of the mountain, Torrie kept watching behind her to make sure she could still see the dim outline of the wagon below on the trail.

There was a good deal of deadfall wood on the ground, and she got an armload quickly, slipping and sliding back down the slope on the wet pine needles, her shoes wet, skirts catching on the upthrust limbs of the fallen trees. She found Cal already back ahead of her, trying to coax fire into some soggy kindling.

Throwing her wood on the ground, she said, "If you'll break this up, I'll get that fire going. It'll take paper to light it in all this dampness."

Climbing into the wagon, she went to her mother's side first, but Liza was still asleep and seemed unchanged. Then, digging under the mattresses, Torrie hauled out one of the boxes of Father's books—it was too bad to use one for this,

193

but it couldn't be helped. At random, she picked up a thin volume and flipped through the pages. As if by long usage they fell open to a certain passage: ". . . So nature pricketh in each one, a courage . . ." Quickly she put that book back and tried another, came up with:

> . . . if a man shall fence his property with 2436 yards of fencing, how many acres . . .

Going back out to the fire, she said, "I found something that will do *fine!*" Rapidly tearing out handfuls of the arithmetic problems, she bolstered the wood with it, and they got the fire started.

With the kettle full of water on to boil, Torrie went back to search the wagon once more, starting with that corner where Liza had kept her secret scraps before. Finally she found them in an old tin box—some dried meat, a handful of old beans bleached white with dryness, a few berries they had gathered along the Truckee, the last of the season, all shriveled and black. There was even a teacup with a bit of lard in it—Mother must have been putting all of her share aside these last weeks! Taking the whole thing back out to the fire, Torrie dumped the scraps, berries and all, into the kettle of water and threw in their last bit of salt for good measure.

With some satisfaction, she said to Cal, "That ought to do Mother some good when it's all boiled up. You keep the fire going while I hunt more wood."

He didn't argue this time, but scowled hard and nodded. "Be careful," he said roughly.

Torrie went a little higher this time, even lost sight of the wagon in the snowfall. It was an eerie feeling to be so detached from every other living thing. As she went about picking up the fallen wood, she glanced around, in time to see something move above her on the hillside. Breathlessly still, she watched for it, and then it moved again—something drifting along up there, from tree to tree. A wolf or a crouched man. . . .

Clutching the wood to her, she turned and went swiftly but quietly back down to where the little burning flicker beckoned her. As she came into the circle of warmth, Cal started up, already sensing her anxiety.

"What is it?" he whispered hoarsely. "Did you see something?"

"I'm not sure," she panted, "but we've got to get the rifle out. You'd better handle it, I don't know how." And then she stopped because Cal was shaking his head with a curious look, rueful and frightened and somehow fatalistic.

"We don't have the rifle," he said.

"We do! Father left it with us this morning—he knew we'd probably drop behind."

"I know, but when he wasn't looking I tied it onto the back of his saddle so he'd have it. I thought up ahead of the train he might see game or something. And besides," Cal grinned feebly, "I thought we should all be brave without any guns, like he said."

They built another fire—a big one—which made warmth on both sides of the cattle. They didn't try to unyoke them, for fear the stock might get away and wander off in the snow. Besides, it would have been a hard job to force the old brindle to its feet. The others had settled themselves too, now, however uncomfortable the yoke may have been. They lay there blinking in the falling snow with the terrible patience of dying animals.

The least they could do, Torrie thought, was try to keep the poor things warm, so she and Cal took turns searching for fuel and feeding the fire. It seemed to eat up the dead-wood with the voracity of a—wolf. She tried not to think about that. Nor could she bear to think of Jess or the Diggers or even of their being all alone. She just kept busy, and understood now why Mother always plunged into some sort of work—less worry and something accom-plished. At least they were fairly warm.

They had both equipped themselves with knives, Torrie with the butcher knife and Cal with Grandpa's big vicious-looking Bowie knife, its naked blade thrust through his belt. She had an impulse to tell him to take care and not cut himself, and then she realized how foolish that would have sounded, when any minute he might be forced to defend his life with that knife.

When the broth seemed as rich as it was going to get, she took a little in a bowl to Liza. Her eyes were open now —she seemed dazed. "What happened?" she asked weakly.

"Nothing," Torrie said soothingly. "You're just tired. Come on and drink some of this."

"Where did you get that?" Her mother struggled to sit up.

"I made it." Torrie pushed her back gently onto the pillows and as Liza ate of it slowly, wonderingly, a little color began to come back to her face.

"You look cold," she said fretfully. "You mustn't get cold, Torrie. The doctor said so. You can't go sleigh-riding. He said if you caught another fever it might go to your lungs—you're so slight-built. He said we should find a warmer place to live, though of course we didn't know it was going to rain and rain—it's still raining, isn't it?"

196

With a shock, Torrie realized that Mother, in her haze of confusion, had given away Father's secret—the real reason for that odd abrupt decision to go west.

"No," she said softly, "it isn't raining and I'm not very cold. I haven't any fever. So go back to sleep, now."

With mingled distress and relief, Torrie got her settled once more under the comforters and saw her drift off again. When she went back outside, she found Cal bringing more wood in the gathering darkness.

"I reckon it's about time Father will be along," he remarked carelessly.

"We're farther behind them than he thinks," Torrie reminded him. "We needn't look for him yet."

"Being the leader is a hard thing, isn't it?" Cal frowned. "I always thought it was the best job, but—" He turned to go and search for wood again. Torrie watched the painful halt in his steps now as he came back with another armload.

"That's enough," she said. "You've done your share. Go on in and get some sleep. I'll take the first watch."

"No, I'm going to stay here with you!" he protested.

"You can't. You've got to be ready to wake up and take over when I get sleepy. Go on now, I'm the captain of this outfit, I just elected myself!" They both tried to laugh at that, but it came out thinly. Without any more argument, Cal hauled himself up into the wagon.

Left alone, with only the drowsing animals and an occasional crack from the fire, Torrie stood a minute listening, trying to sense any danger. She realized all at once that the snow-covered mountains were full of light, and looked up to see the moon riding out of the clouds, which were shredding up and scattering. It was going to be a beautiful night.

Sitting down on the milk stool beside the fire, she thought of that time, a thousand years ago, when she'd wanted to go sleigh-riding and hadn't been allowed. What a fuss she'd put up, and even grumbled about it to Grandpa—how her parents were so cruel! Now that she was able to be honest with herself, she admitted that she'd felt ill all that holiday and hadn't even understood how badly off she was. It was almost the next day that Father had announced this trip. It all fitted perfectly.

The house sold . . . the hard work of preparation . . . Father's saddlesores and the need to buy a cow, which she had hated so at first . . . Cal's broken leg and now Mother, half-starving herself—all of it done for the sake of one complaining little girl. Bitterly she shook her head in disgust at her own blindness. And then that feeling passed and left something much bigger—an overwhelming pride in all of them, a closeness she had never felt before.

Looking down at herself, Torrie saw that, in spite of this rough life, she had picked up and filled out. Her hands were brown and strong, beginning to look like Mother's, and she felt strong inwardly. She felt a purposefulness— the darkness, the silent depths of the mountains with their dangers, couldn't touch her. Her hand tightened on the butcher knife with the fierceness of her intention. So long as those two people slept in there in trust of her, and the fire was needed to guide Father back to them, Torrie felt the towering ability to accomplish anything. And even in this hazardous spot, she had never felt more serene!

II

Torrie roused up, alert at some sound—she heard it again, something or someone coming down the trail. Instinctively, she stood up, her back braced against the wagon. . . .

"Victoria!" The hail came faintly, as if from far out in the darkness, and Torrie went limp with relief and thankfulness. It was Father's voice and the sound along the trail was the crunch of a horse's hoofs in the snow. As he rode into the circle of light, she ran to him, and Thomas slid off Blackie, caught her in his arms, and held her tight.

"I was just at the point of despair when I saw your fires," he told her. "I called out to keep you from being startled —it's so late." He was looking now at the bedded cattle. "Did they give out? I was afraid of something like this, but I did think you'd have made it a little farther. The grade doesn't really begin to steepen for another mile."

Torrie stared at him, shocked. "You mean it gets *worse?*"

"Much worse." Heavily he began to unsaddle the black horse which looked nearly as done in as the rest of the stock. For a week now there had been only the few scattered glades of dry grass where there was any grazing at all.

"I didn't know we were so near the summit," he went on, "but shortly before noon—I was just about to ride back and see how you were coming—we sighted the crest. And at the same time the snow began to fall. What with the steepness, it would have ended all hope of getting across, so we threw every effort into the hastening of the task. With all hands manning the ropes, combining teams and more teams, we managed to haul the wagons the last few hundred yards by main strength. And then—" His face contorted with the memory. "Then I reminded them of our wagon. And . . . they went on. They said . . . it would be dangerous to come all the way back, and they went on."

199

His halting words brought a disastrous sinking inside Torrie, but she tried not to show it as she said, "What will we do then?"

Thomas rubbed his eyes wearily. "That is something for us all to discuss. I think it can wait until morning, though. No need to rouse Caleb and your mother—" He broke off. "What is it, Victoria? Something you haven't told me?"

Reluctantly she recounted everything that had happened since he had left, while a terrible anxiety deepened in his face. She hadn't even finished when he bolted away, into the wagon, leaving the whole image of his fear etched on the silence. Somehow that wordless rush was the last piece of a puzzle that had played itself out all along the trail. Father was as much in love with Mother as she was with him. And love was not a tempest, it was a warmth of nearness or a dry ache of loneliness. . . . Jess. . . .

Intently she made herself think about putting the kettle on the coals to heat. She remembered that Father must not have eaten yet. When he came back out, there was a sorrow in his eyes that frightened her.

"Mother isn't worse?"

He shook his head. "She seems to be in a very deep sleep. It's probably, as you guessed, a case of malnourishment. I had no idea she was depriving herself of food." Almost weakly he sank down onto the three-legged stool. When she put a bowl of soup in his hand, he stared at it as if he didn't know what it was.

"That I should have been gone at such a time," he muttered. "I knew our oxen couldn't make it up the pass, but I kept struggling with the thought of the responsibility I took on when I signed the articles with those people, and I couldn't go back on my word. Naturally I believed that once their wagons were across, they'd bring their teams back to help—"

"Eat some soup," she urged him gently.

"And you did this all alone—the fires—the broth—you were standing guard with that knife!" He looked at her wonderingly.

"Caleb helped. But, Father, you must eat."

Mechanically he did as she told him, and the hot soup seemed to revive him a little. "Thank you, my child—" And then he almost smiled. "No, I can't call you that any more. Find something to sit on and come here beside me. We've a decision to make, you and I."

She brought the milk pail and upturned it, settling herself close to him. Thomas reached out and put a hand on her knee as if to reassure himself. Staring at the fire, he said, "No point in false optimism, Victoria. We're in a bad spot."

"Jess might still come."

"He should have been back long before now," Thomas told her wearily.

"Some of the others thought he might have gone off with our money." Torrie was remembering the odd way Father had looked at Jess that night when he'd volunteered to go ahead. "That couldn't have been why he wanted to go alone?"

"No, certainly not. It was sheer bravery on his part. I shouldn't have let the boy run such a risk, but what else could I do? The rest of the men were—and are—miserable cowards. They'd have added to Jess's burdens rather than been of help. In an emergency they'd have run off and left him, just as they've left us. He wanted to go alone so that he could use his own wits without any hindrances or arguments. I had no alternative but to agree with him. And I'm afraid his courage has cost him his life." He stared into the fire a moment, then shook off his sadness. "But there's no time to grieve, Victoria. We're likely not to fare any better."

Out of the lamentation that had set up silently inside her, Torrie cried, "But at least there are four of us, together."

"Yes, at least that. I'm not sure it's going to make matters any easier."

"What decision did you mean?" she asked. "What must we do?"

He tried to gather himself and speak firmly. "The summit is almost impossibly steep. Even if it were not drifted with snow, we'd never take the wagon over with these tired beasts—not if we had three good teams could we manage it alone. If we leave the wagon here, butcher one of the oxen, and pack as much of the meat as possible on the others, and if they don't all collapse on us from lack of food and if the snow doesn't close in on us again, we might reach the top of the pass on foot tomorrow. How far down the other side we must go before we're out of the freezing weather remains to be seen. I doubt—I seriously doubt—that the cattle can hold up; the dead grass above, if there is any, is under two feet of snow right now. And if they don't make it, we don't. It's that simple."

"What else can we do?" she asked soberly.

"There was a cabin, a short way back down the trail. It seemed to be in fairly good repair. Probably built in the last year or so by some mountain man. We could go back there, butcher all the cattle, and try to dole out the food in such rations that it will last us the winter. If the snows don't linger too long on the ground, we might survive until

202

spring—we'd not be well nourished but we might be alive."
He looked at her, perplexed.

"If you're worried about me, you mustn't be," she said quickly. Then, because he looked so questioning, she went on, "Mother let it slip without realizing it tonight. I know that's why we came west, on account of me. But, Father, I'm better—I feel different."

He smiled and patted her knee with a little affectionate gesture that was so full of his love for her, it made Torrie want to cry, to remember how she'd once thought he didn't care for her.

"That was our immediate reason for coming this year," he admitted, "but there was a greater one. I had felt for some time that our family was pulling apart, becoming hostile to each other for very lack of common sympathy and closeness of interest. I thought we each needed to find some fulfillment, to satisfy ourselves and come to live in peace with each other. But I never perceived in any of my imaginings that we should be brought to such a moment as this, and therein lies the gravest error of all. I believe you when you say you could manage the winter; it's your mother I'm thinking of now. She has apparently seriously weakened herself. And I'm afraid"—he rubbed a hand across his eyes again—"without her strength I admit I feel a little lost."

"If she could decide," Torrie said thoughtfully, "I believe she'd say we must go on."

Thomas seemed to be steadied by the quiet words. He sat silent a moment, then distantly he spoke a line that she remembered from some long time past when he had read his poetry to them. " 'Here is no home, here is but wilderness. . . .' " And then he said, "All right, Victoria. We'll not wait for Fate to catch us, we'll go out and meet it, to-morrow."

And yet in the thin light of morning, with an overcast sky closing in on them again, it was hard to put on an air of confidence. When Cal had learned of the plan, he'd pronounced himself able to walk clear to the Sacramento, but Torrie knew better. His bluff didn't reassure her. Liza seemed a little stronger this morning, she'd eaten the rest of the soup and, though she still looked bewildered, she seemed to understand what they were going to do. However, she accepted Father's explanation with an unnatural passivity and hardly appeared to care that the rest of the train had left them. It was plain to see that she was still not far removed from a state of exhaustion.

The cattle had rested enough to haul the wagon off the trail into the woods a short way, before they were unyoked for the last time.

"That was a good old wagon," Cal said, smacking it with his hand so hard it brought tears to his eyes.

"We'll come back in the spring and get it, God willing," Father told him. "Come along, son, you can help me dispatch this poor ox."

When they'd returned with some parcels of meat and packed them and a few personal belongings on the backs of the other cattle, Father saddled Blackie.

And then, as they started to help Mother up onto the horse's back, she looked around dazed and asked, "Where's Jess?"

It jarred them all. Torrie could see Father wince, and Cal looked thunderstruck.

Gently Thomas said, "Jess hasn't come yet, my dear."

"He hasn't?" Liza's shoulders slackened a little. "I guess I dreamed it, then. I dreamed he came in with some food—"

They got her up onto Blackie and started out, with Father leading him, driving the two oxen and the cow ahead to stamp down the snow and make a track for them to follow. Cal came next, using his crutches to save his leg as much as possible, and Torrie brought up the rear, determined to keep an eye on the boy for the first sign of giving out.

As they walked up the trail in the watery morning light, she looked back once at the wagon, thinking of its boxes of books and linens and dishes, all the familiar household objects that were so much part of her life. For some reason, she thought of a little tin measuring cup that her mother always used and it was harder to leave that than it had been to leave the mahogany bureau. Worse to part with the boxy old high-topped schooner than it had been to leave the house in St. Louis all those months ago. Except that this time she was no wretched weeping child, huddled under a pile of blankets. Turning her back on it, Torrie quickened her pace to catch up to Cal.

At noon they stopped and cooked some of the beef, but they didn't dare take long over it, for the sky was thickening with clouds and a few idle flakes of snow were starting to drift down.

Once, Liza looked up the trail and asked, again, "Is that Jess coming?"

There was no one there, of course. Father sighed deeply. "Not yet, my dear."

Early in the afternoon, the grade began to steepen so that they had to stop and rest the animals every few hundred yards. The snow was falling faster now, making the footing more difficult, and even the horse seemed to be on the point of staggering sometimes. Cal was trying not to limp, but his young face was set with anguish.

Finally Thomas, unable to watch the boy's painful efforts, stopped again. "There's nothing to do but put you on Blackie and trust that—"

"No," Cal gritted between his teeth. "I'm all right. He can't carry double."

And Liza said, for the fifth time, "Is that Jess I see?"

It was almost more than they could bear. Looking around at each other for support, they were silent a minute, and then Torrie answered her mother.

"No—" she began, but automatically she had glanced up the trail and the word died on her lips. Because there was a man riding down toward them—a tall familiar figure in patched clothes and a battered broad-brimmed hat. Riding bareback on a sorrel mare and leading two pack mules.

As Jess reached the speechless little group, his eyes sought out Torrie with the look of a man who has answered some question.

Somehow, he was more silent than ever. As they got out grain for the cattle and everyone was pressing him for a recital of his trip, it seemed to take a long time for Jess to bring himself to talk.

"Yes, sir," he said to Father, "I met your train other side of the hill. They wanted me to turn the supplies over to them. When I saw you weren't along, I figured about what had happened. I gave them a ration of oats for their stock, thought you'd want me to. Then I told them if they wanted a share of the rest, you were still captain of the train, far as I knew, and they could come back over the pass and ask you for it."

But he didn't seem willing to talk about what had gone before. While they stirred up the fire and cooked up another quick meal for themselves, a wonderful meal of fried batter and bacon which he'd brought, it was all they could do to pry the information out of him little by little.

Yes, he'd been jumped by Diggers near where he'd left the note. Chased them off with the Colt revolver.

No, he'd not had much chance to sleep those weeks on the way. Torrie had asked that one; she thought he was looking a good deal thinner than when he'd left them and the pallor under his tan was not just from weariness.

"What about the bones?" Cal wanted to know. And they repeated the story Stanton had told them about the grisly evidence back along the trail.

Jess listened and nodded. To Cal, he said, "That buckskin was really your horse—least I meant him to be. I'm sorry I lost him."

"Then there was truth in the tale!" Father exclaimed.

"Yes, sir. Digger tried to shoot me up yonder as I went over the pass. Lay so flat under his horse one of my shots got it, and one of his arrows got the buckskin."

"But you got him!" Cal ventured eagerly.

Jess didn't smile. "Yes," he said. "I got him." There was a whole unspoken story in the way he spoke, so that all at once Caleb grew straight-faced and subdued and all the rest felt a sympathy as they realized what a terrible thing it had been for Jess, to have to shoot a man.

"We'd better get going," the Virginian said. "Snow's coming on. From the top of the pass, I saw it heading in."

207

As they got ready to set out again, Father lifted Cal onto one of the mules while Jess turned to Torrie. As he looked down at her his face softened. "I'd put you on my mare," he said, "but she's about drug out. The mule's not fancy, but he's been eating regular." Taking her by the waist, he boosted her to the back of the other pack animal, wincing in spite of himself.

Liza, who hadn't said much up to now, spoke up abruptly in her old sharp way. "Jess, you're not well! Were you hurt in that fight?"

He glanced around at them awkwardly. "The reason I'm late getting here, I caught an arrow in my right side, bothered me some. In fact, I had to lay up at Sutter's a while, couldn't sit a horse."

"And shouldn't be sitting one now!" Liza scolded—it did Torrie good to hear her sound natural again.

Jess was shaking his head. "I never did like excuses. You sent me, I should have been back before this. I was almost too late."

Father came over to Jess and held out a hand. As the younger man accepted the grip of it, Thomas said, "You came in good time, son. I'm sure that if you hadn't arrived just when you did, we'd never have made it over the pass." And looking around at them, with an almost naïve gentility, he added, "I really felt this morning that we were embarking upon our last few mortal days. Now I believe we shall cross over an earthly threshold rather than a heavenly one."

DECEMBER

IT WASN'T much of a cabin, but whoever had built it had put in a good big fireplace, and the single room was full of the smell of fresh bread rising and the aroma of roasting goose. The Anders family was going to have a Christmas dinner to top all others!

The goose was a stroke of luck. Caleb, out on the prowl with the rifle, had brought it home last evening. As for the rest of the fare, there would be no sweet potatoes or plum pudding, but they'd make out. They could even laugh about Liza's pots and pans, stowed away up in the Sierras.

Torrie, standing in the doorway in the noonday warmth, thought of other Christmases, the excitement and silliness and foolish preoccupation with presents. There weren't going to be any presents this year and nobody minded at all. It was enough of a gift that they were here and warm, that there was sunlight coming in the door.

And to know that this was their own land—all the way to the river meandering along down there! This American River that wasn't really American yet. It was odd to think that they were on Mexican sod—it *felt* so American. From where she stood, she could see the stock browsing quietly down in the pasture—the two oxen and the cow, Blackie and Jess's mare—all free now to wander and graze at will. All of them were filling out, even though the grass was still dry, waiting to be brought to life by the spring rains which, they said, came so early out here.

> Whenever April with her showers sweet,
> The drouth of March has pierced unto the deep,
> When Zephyr, with his sweet south breath,
> Inspired hath, in every hill and heath,
> The tender crops. . . .

Father kept talking about the farming, taking a wonderful youthful pleasure in the prospect, and Mother was just as full of enthusiasm, trying to remember how they planted, back in the old days on the farm. Neither of them really knew a thing about it, but Torrie was sure now that there was *nothing* they couldn't do. Even Cal, rambling around the hills, looking for rocks bearing gold—she thought he might really find it. Everything seemed marvelously possible.

And then she saw what she'd been watching for—Jess coming. He was far down along the river, but there was no mistaking that blond thatch of hair in the sun. Someone was riding along with him, which was odd—he seldom took up with strangers. He was working now at Sutter's Fort, thirty miles from here, but he came up the river on one of Sutter's horses every time he could get away for a day, and he'd promised for sure to be here for Christmas. Always made it plain that he only came to get his lessons from Father, but Liza was sure it was at least partly her cooking, and Cal thought it was mostly to see the mare. Torrie had her own private ideas.

As she watched him come, she was thinking of what Father had said, back in that hard-pressed moment in the pass—about fulfillment. But suppose your fulfillment is with a man? And you have to wait and wait. . . ? She set herself firmly not to get impatient again as she used to.

They'd turned up the road to the cabin now, the other rider still coming with him. An old man riding a bay mare —somehow it brought her an acute homesickness for Grandpa. He was the one person they were really going to miss this holiday. And then, as they came on, there was something increasingly familiar about that short wiry old figure.

"Mother—" Torrie called uncertainly, "can you come out here—?"

And Liza took just one look, picked up her skirts, and ran to meet them, crying, "Pa! Pa!"

The old man took off his hat and waved it carelessly, as if he'd just ridden over from the farm for a visit.

Later as they all sat around the table only half-tasting the savory dinner, what with all the excitement, Grandpa leaned back, cool as water, and dug into the food handily as he told them his story.

"Got so tarnation lonesome after you left," he said, "I got to figgering I'd take a little jaunt, myself—just over to Liberty to see what was goin' on. Kept hearin' talk about war, you know, folks rushin' around to volunteer. When I got there, that Doniphan was signin' 'em on, all right, and while I ain't sayin' he's not a good soldier, I declare he got not the sense of a wall-eyed jackass when it comes to men. Turned me down fer bein' too old, cuss 'im."

"Pa, you didn't really try to volunteer!" exclaimed Liza, scandalized.

"Why not? I ain't been in a good fight since old Black Hawk give up back in the old days. Made me feel so ornery, bein' shucked off that way, I went along anyhow, with no official title, as you might say. Until they got orders to go clear on whale-spankin' down to Mexico, that's when I quit. Peppery food they got down there prob'ly give me the bellyache. So I heard Kearny was gonna take Santa Fe and I rode on out that way, thought maybe *he'd* got some sense but he didn't. Wouldn't take me neither."

"Oh, Pa!" Mother shook her head.

"Well, 'twasn't much of a fight nohow. I got tired of this kind of fancy-Dan war, everybody makin' speeches, so I come on out along the Gila and across to Californey that way—thought it'd be chilly up north. Come up the coast just takin' my time, wondered where you-all might be at. Then this feller here"—he nodded to Jess—"all the time he's shoein' my horse there at Sutter's and him a friend of yours! I didn't know it until we got talkin' about them folk that's still stuck up there in the pass—them Donners. He mentioned how he'd just come down from there last month, and one thing led to another, and here he is, bringin' me along to find you. Good thing, too." He helped himself to some more goose.

"But, Grandfather," Thomas said, perplexed, "if we'd known you wanted to come west, we'd have been pleased to have you. We thought the trip might be too hard—"

"Hard?" The old man's face cracked into a grin. "Ain't never nothin' hard about what your nature wants to do.

212

Reason I didn't come along with you, I figgered this trip was all your own, and if I'd of come along I'd of been bossin' everybody, because I *know* so tarnation much about everything. From what I heard, you learned somewhat about bossin', yourself."

Father was laughing now along with the others. "Well, sir, when it comes to farming I need a good captain. I hope you'll stay with us. This spring I'm going to try to get a 'tender crop' in the ground."

"Thought your crop was young'uns," snorted Grandpa.

"Well, I hope that will come with time," Father said more seriously, "as the valley fills up and when I can salvage my books from the wagon. But meanwhile I'm going to see what sort of farmer I can become."

The old man looked at him with a glint of admiration. "If you really got the need for a few pointers, reckon I could stay long enough to help you set your furrows straight. Then I figger on findin' me a piece of bottom land alongside this river somewhere and growin' some kitchen vegetables myself. Sutter's got not one good potater to sell in his whole bloomin' store."

"But what about your farm in St. Louis?" Torrie asked.

"Oh that?" Grandpa shrugged. "Before I took this little trip to Liberty, I sold it. It was gettin' old."

Afterward, as Torrie and Jess walked out across the dry winter meadows, she tipped her face up to the late afternoon warmth—she'd only put on a shawl against the evening coolness because of the occasional chill that drifted down from the far-off heights of the Sierras.

"No sign of the Donners yet?" She shivered slightly. "It

must be awful up there now."

Jess nodded. "They tried to take another load of supplies up to them right after we got down, but the snow had closed in—snowed eight days straight," he said. "I guess we were lucky."

"Not lucky!" She turned to him, frowning. "There wasn't any luck about it. First Father saw to it we didn't try to cross the Wasatch, and then you came with food when we were about done in. None of that was luck, unless you might say we were lucky when you hired on with us back in Independence. You drove us and fought for us and saved us, and that isn't what I call luck, Mr. Jess Jessen." All at once, a curious thought came to her. "You know—we still don't even know your first name."

Jess gave her a sidelong glance. "Well, don't think there's anything bad about it," he said. "My ma was a good God-fearin' woman who listened hard to preacher talk and thought she was doing a good thing to give her children a name with some meaning. That's why she named my older brother Fortitude—we called him 'Fort.' And my younger brother's name was Salvation—called him 'Sal.' But there's no good short way to say 'Steadfast-Under-Adversity.' "

"That's—?"

"That's my name. All of it. That's a thing I never meant to tell a soul except the girl I marry, because I knew she wouldn't laugh." He looked at her steadily now. "I'm glad you didn't laugh, Torrie."

"Of course not!" she said indignantly. "Why, it's a perfect name for you, and I—or I mean, your wife—would be very proud of it."

He seemed pleased in a way that went beyond smiling. As naturally as if he'd done it every day of his life, he put an arm around her waist. "Of course, I'm not going to ask you until about ten years from now."

She stared up at him in dismay, only to see him smile a funny unused kind of smile. Torrie realized this was the first time Jess had ever teased her in quite this way—it made her feel warm and close to him. Her arm tightened around his lean waist.

"You'd better not wait too long," she teased back. "When we came through Sutter's there was a girl getting married—she wasn't even sixteen yet. I might get a proposal from some other man myself."

"What would you say?" Jess asked calmly.

"I'd say 'no,' of course!" She laughed and blushed at the same time.

"Good. You say 'no' to a few of 'em and then I'll ask you. If you say 'yes' to me"—he tugged at one of her braids fondly—"I'll know you had a choice, and it'll be a woman who's made up her mind."

And then the teasing was gone between them. Soberly, wishfully, Torrie said, "But it's so far to the Fort—"

"I know, but I've got to make some wages and I've got to spend most of my off-time learning and studying. There isn't enough time," he said restlessly, "not enough time in all the world to learn everything I need to know." In the silence Torrie thought, a little ashamed, of how small a value she had always put on the schooling that had been given her so freely. Silently she vowed to work as hard as Jess this year—he wasn't the kind of man to want a light-minded wife.

"Then," he went on, "when I save up some money, I've got to buy land and build a cabin, start my herd. I couldn't ask a girl to live up over the stable where I bunk now. But

215

I'll be closer by, one of these days. Fellow named Marshall works for Sutter too. Next year he's going to put up a sawmill right here on the American River somewhere, wants me to work on it with him when he gets going, maybe even on shares. I might get rich quicker'n you think. And then—" He looked away out across the valley, and Torrie saw a whole lifetime mirrored in the level thoughtfulness of those blue eyes.

Suddenly he glanced down at her and she became part of those plans—the whole feeling swept over her again, as it always did with Jess. The beautiful feeling.

AFTERWARD

THE TRAGEDY and starvation of the Donners has been told in many places and has left its mark upon the land that trapped them, for the pass still bears their name.

But those cruel wintry days were to be forgotten soon after in a new wild excitement that was to grip the whole country. Shortly after California became American soil, and the American River deserved its name, down in the channel one day, where Jess and the sawmill crew were digging their millrace, John Marshall straightened up with a strange pebble in his hand. It wasn't a stone— it had a dull sheen to it. It was a nugget of gold.